"Leila, I've been invited to Seth and Kylie's wedding on New Year's Eve. Would you like to come with me?"

Her brows rose in surprise. Quinn inviting her to go out with him again was the last thing she'd expected. And, as much as she would have loved to accept, going with him might be a bit obvious. "I've been invited to the wedding too," she admitted. "So I'm sure I'll see you there."

He nodded. "I'll look forward to it."

Pasting a brave smile on her face, she opened the front door. "Goodbye, Quinn."

"Bye, Leila." He looked as if he wanted to kiss her again, but after a brief hesitation he turned and left.

She closed the door, dropping her forehead against the cool wood frame and closing her eyes in a wave of despair.

Maybe it would be best to avoid seeing Quinn again, since she was beginning to think she didn't have the ability to indulge in an affair.

Not without opening herself up to a world of hurt.

Dear Reader

Welcome to **Cedar Bluff Hospital**, located in a small Wisconsin town overlooking the beautiful rocky shores of Lake Michigan. THE SURGEON'S NEW-YEAR WEDDING WISH is the third book in my new mini-series. I really hope you enjoy reading about Quinn and Leila as much as I enjoyed writing about them.

When Leila first meets Quinn in the trauma room, she thinks he's nothing more than an arrogant jerk. But a hidden sorrow in his eyes convinces her there's more to the ED physician than anyone realises. And when Leila meets Danny, Quinn's mute son, she understands the physician's aloofness is nothing more than a way to keep people from getting too close.

A terrible tragedy has robbed his son of the ability to talk, but Quinn is determined that the family-like atmosphere of Cedar Bluff is the best environment to help cure his son. Spending time with beautiful, exotic trauma surgeon Leila Ross isn't part of his plan. But his fierce attraction for Leila is hard to dismiss. What starts out as a sexy fling quickly turns into something far more complex.

The last thing Quinn wants is a wife. Until both he and his son Danny fall head over heels in love with Leila. A new year means new beginnings. Can he convince beautiful Leila to become a part of his family for ever?

I hope you enjoy THE SURGEON'S NEW-YEAR WEDDING WISH. And if you've enjoyed my **Cedar Bluff** mini-series let me know, so I can convince my editor to let me write stories about more **Cedar Bluff Hospital** characters.

Happy Reading!

Laura

THE SURGEON'S NEW-YEAR WEDDING WISH

BY
LAURA IDING

First published in Great Britain 2009
Harlequin Mills & Boon Limited,
Eton House, 18-24 Paradise Road, Richmond, Surrey TW9 1SR

© Laura Iding 2009

ISBN: 978 0 263 20948 8

Set in Times Ron
15-1009-44402

Harlequin Mills &
renewable and rec
sustainable forests
to the legal enviro

Printed and boun
by CPI Antony Rowe, Chippenham, Wiltshire

Laura Iding loved reading as a child, and when she ran out of books she readily made up her own, completing a little detective mini-series when she was twelve. But, despite her aspirations for being an author, her parents insisted she look into a 'real' career. So the summer after she turned thirteen she volunteered as a Candy Striper, and fell in love with nursing. Now, after twenty years of experience in trauma/critical care, she's thrilled to combine her career and her hobby into one—writing Medical™ Romances for Mills & Boon. Laura lives in the northern part of the United States, and spends all her spare time with her two teenage kids (help!)—a daughter and a son—and her husband.

Recent titles by the same author:

EXPECTING A CHRISTMAS MIRACLE*
MARRYING THE PLAYBOY DOCTOR*
EMERGENCY: SINGLE DAD, MOTHER NEEDED
THE SURGEON'S SECRET BABY WISH

Cedar Bluff Hospital trilogy

This book is for you, Olga,
because you've been such a wonderful friend.

CHAPTER ONE

"WHAT do you have for me?" Leila Ross asked, entering the emergency department of Cedar Bluff's hospital. As the trauma surgeon on call, she'd been summoned from her home late on Saturday night, Christmas Day night, in fact—not that she'd made any special plans, aside from a date with her bed, and the sound of her pager had jerked her from a restful sleep.

When she saw the tall, dark-haired ED attending physician standing in the center of the arena, her smile faded and her muscles knotted with tension, starting in her shoulders and moving all the way up her neck.

"Twenty-year-old male with acute abdominal pain in his right lower quadrant," Dr. Quinn Torres said in his lyrical, East Coast voice. If he were any other man, his deep tone and sensual accent might have been attractive. "Elevated white count and acute nausea indicates appendicitis. He's in room eleven."

Despite his Boston accent, Quinn Torres looked Italian with his black hair and olive-toned skin, but his dark eyes made her think maybe his genes had come from Spain or Portugal. Her interest in his heritage was nothing more than pure curiosity, since his face was creased in its usual deep, perpetual scowl.

"Okay, I'll take a look." Leila swept her long straight hair back into a rubber band and quickly washed her hands before approaching the patient. She glanced at his chart. "Jimmy? My name is Dr. Leila Ross and I'm here to evaluate you for possible surgery."

Jimmy Lawton glanced up at her, his green eyes full of pain and an unmistakable hint of fear. "Doc, you have to help me. My stomach hurts so bad I can hardly stand it."

"I will," she promised gently, placing a reassuring hand on his arm and scanning his vital signs before sending Quinn Torres a sharp glance. "Has he been given anything for pain recently?"

"Of course." His haughty voice grated on her nerves. Torres was the newest ED physician on staff, having recently replaced Edward Cagney, who'd retired a few months ago. "He was given 8 milligrams of morphine forty minutes ago."

"I think we'd better give him another dose," she said, tempering her response with an effort. She didn't like Quinn Torres. He was rude, arrogant, aloof and couldn't have been more of an opposite from the rest of the staff at Cedar Bluff, who all radiated warmth and friendliness. He clearly didn't belong here. Even now, the way he stood in the middle of the trauma room, like a king holding court over his subjects, made her want to poke his inflated arrogance with the tip of her scalpel. Why on earth was he here in Cedar Bluff, when a more prestigious hospital was obviously more his style?

She didn't know and didn't really care enough to

ask. Liking or disliking Dr. Torres didn't matter, as she was required to work with him regardless. So far, she couldn't fault the quality of his medical care, even if he did have the personality of a toad. He was meticulous about everything he did, a trait she reluctantly admired since she was very much the same way.

Quinn gave the nurse a nod and she proceeded to give Jimmy another dose of pain medication. Leila tried to ignore Quinn's dark, intense gaze as she continued to examine her patient.

"Have you performed any scans?" she asked, when she finished her physical exam.

"No, I thought I'd wait to see what you required."

Giving an absent nod, she realized she could go either way. A CT scan would be nice, but given Jimmy's young age and the elevated white count she was fairly certain Quinn's diagnosis was correct. The CT scan could be a waste of time and she didn't want a delay to cause his inflamed appendix to burst.

"I'll take him to the OR to explore his abdomen," she decided. "I'll call the supervisor to get the OR crew in."

"I've already ordered the OR crew to come in," Quinn informed her. "They should be here soon, if they haven't arrived already."

His foresight shouldn't have annoyed her, but it did. She told herself to get over it because, really, she was grateful. This way she could take Jimmy into surgery right away. "Thanks," she said, trying to smile. "I appreciate it."

Torres didn't respond and his lack of congeniality only added to her ire. Would it hurt him to be cordial? She spent a few minutes explaining the procedure to

Jimmy, ordered a dose of antibiotics and then asked Susan, the nurse, to get her patient prepped to go upstairs. She turned and reached for the chart at the same time Quinn did and as their fingers tangled, a jolt of heat sizzled all the way down her spine.

"Excuse me," he said stiffly, turning away at the same moment she'd snatched her hand back. Struggling to calm her racing heart, she stared at his retreating back, stunned by her unexpected, and unwanted, visceral reaction to the man she intensely disliked.

"Do you need anything else, Dr. Ross?" Susan asked, handing over the antibiotic she'd requested.

Leila successfully pulled her attention firmly back to the patient. "No, thanks, Susan. Let's go." Leila placed the chart on the bed and helped push Jimmy's gurney upstairs, still slightly shaken by that brief, electrifying touch. No doubt she'd totally imagined it. She'd been physically and emotionally exhausted this past week, the anniversary of her husband's death hitting her harder than she'd expected. Even though George had died two years ago, she still missed him.

She'd loved her husband, even if their marriage had been too brief. George Ross had been a wonderful, kind and gentle man. There was no way she was even remotely attracted to a guy like Torres. Absolutely not.

As they reached the OR, she left Jimmy in very capable hands while she took time to scrub, resolutely pushing those irksome thoughts away and focusing every iota of her attention on the patient who needed her care.

Refusing to waste another second thinking about Quinn Torres.

* * *

Leila finished operating on Jimmy Lawton, thankfully catching his engorged appendix before it ruptured, only to receive another trauma call. Wryly preparing herself for a long night, minus any sleep, she hustled back down to the ED.

She was surprised to see Quinn was still there. Hadn't his shift ended at eleven? Apparently not, since he was currently giving orders in a harsh tone that reminded her of a marine drill sergeant.

"What's going on?" she asked, stepping into the trauma bay. There was a lot of blood surrounding the male patient lying on the gurney, and she could tell he was bleeding from his head, nose and mouth, not to mention the places she couldn't see, like internally. Two nurses pumped blood and fluid on a level-one rapid infuser while another one scurried to get blood for additional lab work.

"He took a swan dive off the roof of his parents' two-story house, leaving behind a suicide note. He hit the concrete driveway from an estimated distance of twenty feet." The pertinent details didn't come from Quinn, but from the charge nurse. "Took the brunt of the force on his legs, which might be the only reason he's still alive."

Oh, boy, she hated jumpers. They were the worst because the trauma was often so severe there wasn't much chance of survival. Why couldn't he have hit the snow-covered ground instead? At least then he'd have a better chance.

What a horrible Christmas memory for his parents.

"Leila, he needs to get to the OR, stat," Quinn said when he saw her. The grimly fierce expression on his face surprised her, no sign of his cool arrogance now. "He's losing blood faster than we can pump it in and I'm certain he's bleeding internally."

She was certain of that, too, but this patient's status as a viable candidate for the OR wasn't quite as clear. "What's the extent of his head injury?" she asked.

"Pupils fixed and dilated. He wasn't found right away, not until one of his friends kept trying to get in touch with him and called the parents," Mary, the charge nurse, told her. "Their bedroom is on the other side of the house and they didn't hear him hit the ground."

"Fixed and dilated pupils are a bad sign. He needs a neurosurgical consult," Leila told Quinn.

"I've called them and they're on their way, but he has skull fractures, so there's a chance he won't suffer brain death. He needs to go to the OR immediately." Quinn's intense insistence was very unlike him. Where was his cool detachment?

Upon examining the patient closer, she realized his legs appeared firm and unnaturally taut. Compartment syndrome, bleeding into the tissue around the bone, was a serious, life-threatening complication of multiple trauma. "What is his tissue perfusion pressure?" she asked sharply.

Quinn shook his head, indicating he hadn't checked it.

Leila glanced at the nurse. "Get me the Stryker STIC monitor, we need to know what his tissue perfusion levels are."

"Draw a myoglobin level and a lactic acid level, too," Quinn added, quickly realizing the danger.

She set up the monitor and then inserted a needle into the patient's muscle. Quinn leaned over to see the reading for himself.

"We're losing his blood pressure," one of the nurses running the rapid infuser warned. "Do you want more blood or saline?"

"Both," Leila and Quinn responded at the same time.

"Two more units of blood and one liter of fluid," Quinn clarified. "Make sure you have his vasopressors turned up as high as possible."

"Tissue perfusion pressures are elevated at 38 millimeters of mercury," Leila said, glancing at Quinn. "I'll take him to the OR for a stat fasciotomy in both legs and I'll explore his belly, too. But it's likely that this massive fluid resuscitation isn't helping his brain injury at all, so you must realize his prognosis is poor."

"I know." Quinn's dark eyes were grim, haunted, as if he was taking this young man's fate directly to heart. "I'll talk to his parents. Please do your best."

"I will." Leila turned and quickly gave orders for the patient to be moved up to the OR.

Her adrenaline was pumping, heightening her awareness as she prepared for surgery. The young man's name was Anton Mayer and as she finished her scrub and entered the OR, she noticed his condition wasn't any better. In fact, if anything, he looked worse.

Feeling slightly sick to her stomach, Leila reached for her scalpel. She was going to keep her promise to Quinn and do everything possible, but she had an awful feeling that Anton was going to die.

Not yet, she reminded herself grimly, doing the fasciotomy to both lower extremities first and then preparing to explore his abdomen. He wasn't going to die yet.

But after working on his legs, she moved to his abdomen and when she saw he had a severely fractured kidney, she knew things were worse than she'd feared. She took the damaged kidney out but the bleeding was profuse. She could barely see where the source of the bleeding was coming from in the sea of blood.

"We're losing him," Dirk Greenfield, the anesthesiologist, warned. "I can't sustain his blood pressure."

"Keep trying," Leila said, praying she could find the source of his bleeder. Although there was likely more than one source. Sweat dampened the back of her scrubs, running down the sides of her face. She tried to tackle one emergency at a time.

"Blood pressure is gone, he's in PEA."

PEA was pulseless electrical activity, which basically meant the kid was bleeding to death. Or he'd already herniated his brain from all the fluids they'd given during the trauma resuscitation.

"Bolus him with epi, I found the arterial bleed." At least she'd found one of them, though she suspected there could be more.

"I already bolused him with epinephrine several times. Now he's in a wide complex rhythm."

"No!" Leila didn't so much as glance at the heart monitor, keeping her gaze focused on what she was doing. One more stitch and she'd have the artery closed off. Then she could take a look at his spleen. Maybe that was the other major source of his bleeding.

Finishing with the artery, she quickly switched the focus of her exploration on the area of his spleen, cutting the splenic artery in an effort to minimize the blood loss. But once the artery was open, she realized the blood wasn't pulsing at all, but simply oozing at a slow rate.

Horrified, she glanced up at the monitor, realizing it was too late.

"Didn't you hear me, Leila?" Dirk asked. "I said he's gone."

She momentarily squeezed her eyes closed and dropped her chin to her chest. She hadn't heard, hadn't wanted to believe what her professional eyes were telling her. After taking a moment to compose herself, she lifted her head and glanced at the clock. "Time of death 1:32 a.m."

There was nothing more they could have done. She knew it, yet that didn't make the prospect of telling Anton's parents that their seventeen-year-old son was dead any easier.

When she returned to the ED, Quinn immediately crossed over, although he stopped abruptly when he saw by her expression that the news wasn't good.

"I'm sorry," she said in a weary tone. "I did the bilateral fasciotomies, but he had a severely fractured kidney, a ruptured spleen and so much other internal damage along with his head injury that I just couldn't save him."

Quinn stood there for a long moment, his jaw clenched, his gaze dark and resigned as he gave a brief nod. "I'll talk to his parents."

She wasn't sure why, maybe because he seemed to be taking the news so hard, but she reached out to touch him. "I'm the surgeon of record. I should do it."

As still as a statue, he stared at her hand on his arm

as if it was something he'd never seen before and then finally raised tortured eyes to hers. "We'll both go," he said in a low, gruff voice.

Surprised by his acquiescence, she simply nodded and walked alongside him to the small private waiting room he'd given to the boy's parents, not far from the larger public one.

His mother took one look at them and promptly burst into tears.

Quinn opened his mouth, but no sound emerged from his throat. He swallowed hard and sent Leila a silent plea for help.

Leila stepped up. "My name is Dr. Ross. I took Anton for emergency surgery, but he had too many injuries, to his spleen, his kidneys and his brain. I'm so sorry to tell you, he's gone."

"No-o-o," wailed the mother, collapsing onto her husband for support. When Anton's father broke into harsh sobs, his large shoulders shaking with grief, Leila felt her own eyes well up, too.

This part of her job never got any easier. Never.

"Why did he do this?" Anton's mother asked. "Why?"

Again she had no answers. She glanced toward Quinn, whose face was drawn so tight he almost looked angry, but the agonized expression in his gaze reinforced his struggle to hide his own grief and helplessness.

"It's not your fault," Quinn finally said, taking a step forward to put a reassuring hand on the sobbing woman's shoulder. "Please know, this isn't your fault."

"It has to be our fault!" The woman cried, nearly incoherent in her distress. "How could we not have known he was so unhappy? How could we have missed it?"

"It's not your fault," Quinn repeated.

"Teen suicide is very tragic," Leila said in a soft tone, picking up a pamphlet from the rack of educational brochures on the wall. "It's normal to feel responsible, but you need to know Dr. Torres is right. This isn't your fault." She slid the pamphlet toward Anton's mother. "There's a support group here for parents just like you. When things calm down after a few weeks, please consider giving them a call."

Anton's mother continued to cry and didn't take the brochure. Anton's father pulled himself together, the gut-wrenching sobs eventually quieting, and he reached for the information, folding the pamphlet before sliding it in his pocket. Leila sincerely hoped they'd get the help they needed.

After a few more minutes, she and Quinn left them alone. The ED nurses would keep an eye on the parents and for now their job was over.

"That was a rough one," Leila murmured to Quinn. "He was so young."

"Any suicide is rough, regardless of how young the patient is," Quinn said in a harsh tone. "Suicide is a horrible thing to do to a family."

Shocked by his outburst, she didn't know what to say.

Instantly, his face changed, resuming the remote, cold mask he normally wore. "Excuse me, but I need to make rounds on the other patients in the arena."

He left and Leila stared after him, the brief moment of camaraderie between them having vanished in a heartbeat.

Yet she wasn't angry or upset. As she watched him move toward the arena and speak to the charge nurse, she found herself wondering about the enigmatic physician.

Because she was fairly certain Quinn Torres wasn't nearly as arrogant and rude as she'd originally thought.

She was beginning to realize his outward aloofness might be a shield to hide the suffering he was feeling inside.

CHAPTER TWO

QUINN tried not to dwell on Anton Mayer's death as he finished the remainder of his work and prepared to head home. He'd split the night shift with Jadon Reichert who'd come in to relieve him at three in the morning to cover Simon Carter's holiday. It was only fair, as Simon had worked the night shift on Christmas Eve.

Physically exhausted and emotionally drained, he crawled into bed, hoping to get at least four hours of sleep before he had to get up to face the day.

Yet as soon as he closed his eyes, the image of Anton's bloody face bloomed in his mind. Squeezing his eyes tight and trying to push it away didn't help because he could still hear the desperate sobs of Anton's parents echoing through the room as Leila told them Anton was gone.

The young man's death haunted him.

He didn't need a psychiatrist to explain why. He knew full well the events of the night reminded him too much of his wife, Celeste. She hadn't jumped off a two-story building onto concrete, but she'd died by her own hand just the same, abruptly ending her young life far too soon.

He'd resented reliving the grief and angst all over again while talking to Anton's parents. Knowing you should have saved someone and hadn't was an awful feeling. He'd known exactly what dark hopelessness they'd felt.

Thank heavens for Leila. He wasn't sure what he would have done if she hadn't come with him. She'd been the one who'd given them the bad news. And she'd also cried with them, while he'd stood and helplessly watched.

And then she'd tried to comfort him, and he'd snapped at her. He'd learned in the months since Celeste's death that rudeness and arrogance kept people away.

So why did he regret the way he'd spoken to Leila?

Scrubbing his hands over his face, wishing he could erase the scars of the past as easily, he stared through the darkness up at the ceiling. He owed the beautiful, exotic surgeon a debt of gratitude. And an apology. She hadn't deserved the harsh edge of his anger.

Thinking of Leila helped him to forget about Anton, at least temporarily. Those few moments when their fingers had tangled over the chart had sent his pulse sky-rocketing into triple digits. The physical reaction, akin to being poked with a laser-tipped bovie, had startled him. He hadn't felt anything remotely like it in the many months since Celeste's death.

Leila was a good surgeon, he'd figured that out shortly after working with her the very first time. And she was the one who'd noticed Anton's compartment syndrome in his legs. He didn't blame her for not being able to save the young man. He'd known right from the first that Anton's chances of surviving his severe injury had been slim.

Leila's ability to be compassionate with her patients and their families, while maintaining her professionalism, was a trait he admired.

Yet admiring the woman was one thing, being interested in her on a personal level was completely out of the question. Certainly she was beautiful, her ethnicity portraying a hint of the Orient, with her slightly almond-shaped eyes and straight black hair. But he'd been surrounded by beautiful women before and hadn't once felt even a flicker of interest.

Testosterone, he thought as exhaustion weighted his eyelids. He was a man who'd been celibate for too long and she was a beautiful woman. His response to her had been nothing more than chemistry, plain and simple.

Nothing more.

A gentle, yet insistent patting on his chest caused Quinn to rouse from sleep. He swallowed a groan and groggily opened his eyes, realizing he was not alone.

His six-year old son, Danny, was patting his chest, silently asking him to wake up. He swiped the grit from his eyes and smiled at him. "Good morning, Danny," he said, hoping but not expecting a response.

Danny grinned, showing a small gap between his two front baby teeth. His son signed the word *breakfast* and Quinn nodded.

"Yes, I'm hungry for breakfast, too." He automatically signed the words, even though he knew perfectly well there was nothing wrong with Danny's ability to hear. Still, if he didn't practice his signing, he tended to get rusty. "Where's Auntie D.?"

In the kitchen, making oatmeal, Danny signed in response. *She wants to know if you want some, too.*

"Sure." He might have preferred eggs and bacon, but Celeste's aunt, Delores Newkirk, had been on a major health food regimen lately, so he suspected fried eggs and bacon were not an option. He was so grateful that she'd stepped up to help him with Danny, agreeing not only to taking care of his son during whatever chaotic hours he had to work but also relocating with them from Boston to the tiny town of Cedar Bluff, that he'd decided long ago not to complain. He couldn't imagine raising his son without the help of the plump, middle-aged godsend, the one member of his wife's family who didn't blame him for Celeste's death, although he certainly understood their feelings. "Just give me a few minutes to shower and I'll be ready."

Danny grinned again. *Okay, but you'd better hurry 'cause oatmeal tastes bad when it's cold.*

"Right." He nodded in agreement, swinging his legs out of bed and wishing there was an easy way to mainline caffeine. He needed to blow the cobwebs from his brain. The scent of coffee teased him mercilessly as he made his way to the shower.

Fifteen minutes later, he padded into the kitchen, where Delores was seated at the kitchen table across from Danny. "Good morning, Quinn. Did you have a rough night?"

"Not too bad," he said with a shrug, making a beeline for the coffeemaker. "Thanks for making breakfast."

"You came home pretty late," she commented. Her

tone was casual, but the glint in her eye betrayed her interest. "Did you go out after your shift?"

Quinn hid a sigh. Lately, Delores was becoming obsessed with his social life or lack thereof. He was growing weary of her not-so-subtle hints. "No, the night shift physician worked Christmas Eve night, so I split the shift with the day shift doctor to cover the night shift for Christmas night. I stayed until three in the morning and Jadon came in at three."

"Oh." She wrinkled her nose in disappointment. Then her expression brightened. "But you're off the rest of the day, right?"

"Yes, and so are you." He took a seat next to her at the table and helped himself to the large bowl of oatmeal she'd set out for him. "You're going down to Chicago for a holiday visit with your sister today, and don't pretend you've forgotten."

"But I don't have to go if you need me to stay here," she said, rising to her feet to refill her coffee mug. "Cynthia would surely understand if Danny needs me to stay."

"Hardly," he muttered, unable to imagine his wife's mother caring one way or the other about the grandson she hadn't seen in well over a year. Her anger toward Quinn at causing her daughter's death had unfortunately carried over to his and Celeste's son. He felt bad for Danny, not himself. "In fact, if you don't go, she'll blame me for that, too."

Delores sighed and nodded. "I guess you're right. But what about next weekend? Surely you can make some plans to go out next weekend?"

"I'll think about it," Quinn said evasively. Next

weekend was New Year so it was unlikely he'd make special plans for then, either. He turned toward his son, who was listening intently to their conversation. "So, Danny, what would you like to do today? Are you ready for another video game challenge?"

You didn't forget about sledding, did you? Danny signed, his eyes widening in alarm.

"Sledding?" Quinn repeated in confusion. He glanced questioningly at Delores.

"The sledding party is later this afternoon," Delores clarified, doing as Quinn did, signing and talking. She sent Quinn an apologetic glance. "Ah, do you have a sled for him to use?"

"No, but we can run to the store later," Quinn said. He smiled at his son. "How about we play video games for a while first, then we'll go buy a sled?"

Danny nodded vigorously. *Okay. But you know I always beat you when we play.*

Quinn laughed. "Not this time. I've been practicing when you've been asleep."

Danny flashed him a pitying look that clearly indicated he didn't believe him as he slid down from his seat and carried his empty oatmeal bowl over to the sink. *Hurry up*, he signed before darting into the living room.

"Do you think it's a good idea to encourage those video games?" Delores asked once Danny had left. "After all, those games aren't going to encourage him to talk."

"He'll talk when he's ready," he said, repeating what Dr. Nancy Adams had told him. Nancy was a semi-retired speech pathologist who'd graciously agreed to take Danny's case when Quinn had explained the circumstances around his son's traumatic muteness. He'd relocated to Cedar Bluff just for the chance to have Danny work with her. Of course, the small-town feel of Cedar Bluff was pretty nice, too. At least so far the kids in Danny's first-grade class hadn't begun to ridicule him.

"I hope you're right," Delores said, before getting up from the table. "I guess I'll get ready to go visit my sister, unless you've changed your mind?"

"Go on, you deserve some time away from here," he urged.

Delores left him to finish his oatmeal in peace. As he enjoyed the maple and brown sugar flavor he thought about Danny. He trusted Nancy's knowledge and skill, yet at the same time he'd begun to despair that his son would ever speak again. The kids his age welcomed him into their group now, but what would happen in a few years? Kids could be incredibly cruel, and generally those who were "different" took the brunt of the teasing.

He couldn't bear the thought of Danny becoming ostracized by the other kids because of his self-imposed silence.

With a weary sigh, he shoved the troubling thoughts aside, finished his breakfast and stood, cleaning up the mess from their meal before going to join his son in the video game challenge.

All he could do for now was to wait and see. Hopefully, Dr. Adams would find the key to unlock Danny's voice.

That afternoon was bright and sunny, perfect weather for sledding, and Quinn found himself standing awkwardly next to several other parents at the Cedar Bluff sledding hill. Since he was still relatively new to the area, and worked odd hours, he didn't know most of them, not even by sight, especially because Delores was the one who picked up Danny from school. The only familiar face belonged to Seth Taylor, one of the emergency department attending physicians.

Quinn tended to avoid small talk, hating having to answer all the questions that invariably followed the moment people realized Danny was mute. He generally used his bluntness to keep people away, not wanting his personal life to become the source of small-town gossip.

Instead, he kept his eye on his son. Danny was having a great time, sledding down the hill in his new plastic bright blue sled. Quinn noticed that two of the boys, Ben Germaine, who was Seth's fiancée's son, and Charlie Atkins, another boy in their class, acted very friendly toward Danny, as if they didn't care about his lack of speech.

"Come on, Danny. Let's ride together!" Charlie said excitedly.

Danny eagerly nodded and climbed onto his blue sled, moving up to the front and indicating with gestures for Charlie to climb on the back. The sound of Charlie's young, carefree laughter rang through the air as they started down the hill.

A slight smile tugged at the corners of Quinn's mouth as he gazed after the boys. It was times like this that he was glad he'd made the move to Cedar Bluff. He was grateful that Danny had already found some friends. Maybe Cedar Bluff didn't have the same lure for adults as Boston, but as far as he was concerned Danny's well-being was all that mattered.

He frowned, though, when Danny's blue sled veered off course, turning sharply to the right, heading directly toward a line of trees.

"Danny!" he shouted, through cupped hands, taking several steps forward. "Watch where you're going!"

He couldn't tell what happened. It seemed as if the boys were somehow tangled up on the sled and not steering at all because the lightweight plastic sled gathered speed as it shot down the slippery slope toward a large oak tree.

"Danny!" Quinn shouted again, running down the hill toward his son, feeling helpless when he realized he wasn't going to make it in time. *"Danny!"*

Too late. The sled hit the tree with enough force to knock both boys sprawling into the snow.

Leila finished her lunch in the ED staff break room and leaned back against the sofa cushions, momentarily closing her eyes. Only another twenty-four hours and her long weekend call rotation would be over. At least today should be relatively quiet—it wasn't exactly a party night of the week, compared to Friday and Saturday. The holiday weekend couldn't end soon enough. She was exhausted, the steady stream of patients had been unusual considering it was Christmas.

She sighed, thinking she would just rest for a few more minutes. What seemed like a nanosecond later, a hand on her shoulder caused her to jerk upright, and she realized Jadon Reichert, the ED attending physician on duty, was trying to wake her up.

"What?" she asked groggily, trying to shake off her lethargy. Disoriented, she blinked away her blurred vision to focus on the large wall clock, noting with shock that she'd slept for more than an hour and a half.

"Leila? Sorry to bother you but we have two peds traumas on the way in," Jadon said, his expression apologetic for needing to rouse her.

"Sorry, didn't mean to fall asleep," she muttered, pushing herself upright.

"Hey, no problem," Jadon said with a wry grin. "I'd cover the rest of your shift for you, but I think hospital administration might frown on me for performing surgery without the proper credentials."

She had to chuckle as she rose to her feet. "Yes, they probably would. Okay, I'm really awake now. What's coming in? Did I hear you say we have two peds traumas?"

Jadon's smile faded, his gaze turning serious. "Two young boys hit a tree while sledding at Cedar Bluff Park."

Leila frowned, her stomach clenching in warning. This was one of the reasons she was glad she'd decided not to have kids. "Please tell me one of them isn't Ben Germaine."

"No, not this time," Jadon assured her. "Although it sounds as if Seth Taylor was on the scene, along with Quinn."

Quinn? How odd. But she didn't give the coincidence more than a passing thought.

"Thank heavens Ben wasn't involved." Ben was Kylie and Seth's son and the boy tended to be a bit accident prone. Earlier that month, he'd slipped on the rocks and tumbled into the icy water of Lake Michigan. Jadon's new fiancée, Alyssa, had fallen in herself, when trying to save him. She'd been pregnant at the time, seven and a half months along with twins. Leila had been there when they'd been brought in and it was touch and go for a while. Thankfully, everyone was fine now, including Jadon and Alyssa's twin girls, Grace and Gretchen, born several weeks early. The entire incident had been very scary, touching many of the Cedar Bluff staff members who'd been concerned when one of their own had been injured.

Technically, Ben was Kylie's son, but it was clear from Seth's actions that he already considered the boy to be his own. Seth and Kylie were getting married next weekend, on New Year's Eve.

She envied their happiness, although reminded herself that she'd been lucky to have loved a wonderful man like George. George had understood and respected her hesitancy to have children, considering she didn't know anything about her heritage. Heaven knew what genes she'd be passing on. She missed him, and tried to be grateful for the few months they'd shared together.

Pushing the sorrows of the past aside, Leila was going to ask more details about their young patients, but in that moment both their pagers went off.

"They're here," he said, leaving the staff break room in a rush to get out to the trauma room. Leila followed close on his heels, her previous exhaustion quickly submerged beneath a fresh wave of adrenaline.

"Danny is the more seriously injured of the two," Kylie Germaine was saying, as the gurneys were wheeled in. Leila was surprised to see Quinn Torres walking on the opposite side of the gurney from Kylie, hanging on to the boy's hand. What on earth had he been doing on the sledding hill? "Danny is six years old, weighs an estimated thirty pounds and has sustained a head injury and possible fractured left tibia."

"And what about the second victim?" Leila asked, not willing to take only the paramedic's word about which patient was worse, no matter how much she liked and trusted Kylie. She needed to make her own judgment.

Quinn opened his mouth, but Kylie put a hand on his arm and continued, not giving him the chance to interrupt.

"Charlie Atkins is also six years old, also estimated to be about thirty pounds and he doesn't seem to have any obvious signs of injury," Kylie informed them. "Charlie's vitals are stable. Danny Torres was in the front of the sled and took the brunt of the force when they hit the tree."

Danny Torres? Leila suppressed a spurt of surprise in discovering Quinn had a son. She never would have guessed him to be a father. Did Quinn have a wife, too?

And why did she care?

Her gaze centered on the boy. Danny was crying, but not making much noise, his sobs choked as if he was afraid to make any sound. Her heart melted in empathy. She crossed over to him, trying to ignore Quinn's sharp, penetrating gaze.

"Hi, Danny, my name is Dr. Leila and I'm here to help make you feel better." She gave Danny her best reassuring smile and the boy struggled to stop crying, seemingly listening to her soft voice. "You're being very brave, Danny. I know you're hurt. The nurse is going to give you something to take away your pain, but first I need to ask you a few questions. Can you tell me exactly where it hurts the most? Which part of your body hurts the most?"

Danny pointed to his left leg and looked up at his father, tears continuing to trickle silently down his ruddy cheeks.

"No, Danny can't tell you where it hurts," Quinn said in a low, rough voice full of parental concern. "He doesn't talk, but he does know sign language. I'll translate for him."

CHAPTER THREE

"DANNY doesn't talk?" Leila said with a frown. That didn't make sense, since Danny seemed to hear her just fine. Unless he was extremely skilled at lip-reading? "I'm sorry, I didn't realize he was deaf."

"He's not deaf," Quinn said in a clipped, irritated tone. "He just doesn't talk." Quinn's jaw was tense as if he didn't like having to explain his son's situation. He turned toward the boy and his voice became gentle. "Danny, Dr. Ross wants to know where you hurt. Tell us exactly what hurts you, okay?"

Danny pointed to his left leg and his forehead. He had the same jet-black hair as his father, and the same dark compelling eyes. The resemblance between father and son was striking.

"What about your stomach, Danny?" Leila persisted. "Does your stomach hurt? Or maybe your ribs?"

Danny shook his head, big, fat tears trickling down his cheeks. For some reason, those silent tears bothered her more than if he'd been wailing loudly. Kylie had stabilized his left lower leg, containing his possible fracture within an inflatable boot, but for the moment she was more concerned about the extent of his head injury. "Okay, Danny, I'm going to examine you for a minute here. I'm going to flash a small light into your eyes, okay? Can you look over my shoulder at the wall behind me?"

Danny nodded and complied with her request. His pupils were unequal but did react to light. "Any blurred vision, Danny? Or ringing in your ears? Do you feel sick to your stomach?"

Quinn's son shook his head to all her questions.

She could feel Quinn's intense gaze and couldn't help wondering if he didn't trust her judgment. At least, not when it came to his son.

"Danny, can you tell me where you are?" To this point, she'd given him all yes or no questions, but now she needed to really assess his brain function. "What is this place?"

"Hospital," Quinn said when Danny made a few graceful gestures with his small hands. "The hospital where my dad works."

"Good. Now, tell me which holiday we just had?"

For a moment the boy's forehead furrowed, as if he had to think about her question.

She glanced at Quinn. "Do you celebrate the holiday?"

Quinn nodded. "Which holiday did we just have, Danny?" he asked, signing the question at the same time.

"Christmas," Quinn said when Danny responded by signing again. "He says he received a games console for Christmas."

"Ah, I bet that's fun. I heard Ben Germaine got one,

too. Do you let your dad play with it or is it only for kids?" she asked.

For the first time, a smile broke through on Danny's young face. He nodded, his fingers flew again and she found herself wishing she knew sign language herself, so she could communicate better with the boy directly, without needing Quinn.

"Yes, he lets me play so that he can win," Quinn translated.

She laughed. "Good for you, Danny. I'd love to watch you beat your dad. Now, is it okay if I listen to your heart and lungs?"

Danny nodded, and she quickly auscultated his heart, lungs and stomach before straightening to glance at Quinn.

"He certainly seems stable, but with his pupils being slightly unequal in size, I'd like to get a CT scan of his head, just to make sure we're not missing anything more serious. We can also get the X-rays of his leg at the same time. I'd like to have the films ready before I call the orthopedic surgeon on call to take a look at his leg."

"All right," Quinn said, giving his consent. "I'd like to go with him to the radiology department."

"Of course. And we'll give him something for pain, too, since I'm sure his leg will be hurting once they take that boot off." For an awkward moment she hesitated, wondering if she should ask about Danny's mother or not. Quinn wasn't exactly forthcoming about his personal life. He was dressed casually, in a pair of black jeans and a black sweater, and she'd noticed he wasn't wearing a wedding ring, which didn't necessarily mean a whole lot these days. "Is there…anyone else you'd like us to notify?"

"No." Quinn's response was blunt.

Danny was frowning and he tugged on his father's arm to get his attention. The boy signed a question. She watched with a puzzled frown, wondering what was wrong.

"If I call Auntie D., she'll cut her visit short," Quinn said to Danny's silent question. She noticed Quinn signed and spoke to Danny at the same time, regardless of the fact that Danny could hear. "I'll call her later on to let her know what happened, okay?"

"Auntie D.?" Leila repeated, knowing full well she was poking her nose into his personal business yet unable to help herself.

Quinn hesitated, as if he might not answer, but then said, "Danny's caregiver. She's really Danny's great-aunt, she helps look after Danny while I'm at work."

"I see." So there was an Auntie D. in the picture, but no mother. She wanted to ask more, but this wasn't the time as she still needed to call Radiology to get the CT scan and X-rays, and check out her other patient. "Give me a few minutes to get the radiology exams ordered."

When she'd finished making all the arrangements, she crossed over to where Jadon was examining Charlie. "How is he?"

"Fine. I can't find any major signs of injury other than maybe a sprained wrist."

"Great." She smiled at Charlie. "Guess you're pretty lucky, huh? At least you won't be stuck in a cast, like Danny will be."

Charlie frowned at the news. "I think my wrist needs

a cast, too," he said in a serious tone, holding up his injured wrist. "It hurts really, really bad."

"Hmm." She hid a smile and pretended to consider his words as she gently manipulated his wrist. "We could put an immobilizer on for a few days, it's not as bulky as a cast but it should work to keep the pain and swelling down. But that means you won't be able to play any video games."

"No video games?" Charlie's eyes widened comically as he realized the impact of his request.

"Nope." She took a small wrist immobilizer from the cart even though they generally didn't like to use them because some exercise was good for mildly injured joints, but she wasn't worried because she suspected this particular immobilizer wouldn't last on Charlie's wrist for very long anyway. She placed it over his sore wrist. "Now, you should wear this during the day, but once your wrist starts to feel better, you can take it off."

"Okay." Charlie seemed satisfied with the compromise. His mother rushed in and he proudly held up his wrist. "Mom, I got a sprain!"

"A sprain? Let me see." The woman examined his wrist, then put a hand on her son's head, checking for other signs of the sledding crash. She gave Leila a harried glance. "Does he have any other injuries? Is he really all right?"

"Yes, he's fine." Leila gave her a reassuring smile. "And he can take off the immobilizer once his wrist begins to feel better or once he's tired of wearing it. You're just in time as he's all ready to be discharged home."

"Thank heavens," Charlie's mother muttered, giving

him a quick hug. "Don't ever scare me like that again, do you hear me?" she said to her son.

"I won't. But can I see Danny before I go?"

Leila glanced over to where Quinn and Danny were still waiting to head over to the radiology department. "Yes, I'm sure Danny wouldn't mind if you went over to say goodbye."

Charlie scrambled down from the gurney with a guiding hand from his mother and went over to his friend. Danny didn't speak and Charlie didn't know sign language, but it was clear to her that the boys still managed to communicate with each other just fine between Charlie's words and Danny's gestures.

Moments later, the transport team came to pick up Danny for his tests.

"Let's get this place cleared up. We'll put Danny in a regular room in the arena when he gets back," Leila said to Amy, the nurse in charge for the day.

"Okay. What do you think is wrong with Danny that he won't talk?" Amy asked, as she began to clear the area.

"I don't know and it's not any of our business one way or the other," Leila said in a tone meant to squash the rumor mill. She headed over to the nearest workstation to finish documenting Danny's assessment.

Although as she completed the necessary paperwork, she couldn't help wondering the same thing. Why on earth didn't Danny talk? Especially if he could hear and understand perfectly well?

Since Quinn had purposefully kept quiet about Danny's situation, she figured he wasn't going to tell her just to satisfy her idle curiosity.

It was an hour and a half later before Danny's leg was put in a cast, the X-rays having revealed a clean break in his left tibia. The bright lights had started to bother him, though, so as soon as the boy's cast had been applied, Quinn had shut down the lights.

Leila entered the room, holding the report containing Danny's CT scan results. "Danny's CT scan is clear, Quinn, but I have to tell you, I'd feel better if we kept an eye on him here overnight. Jadon agrees with me on this."

Quinn read the results and then glanced down at Danny. "I don't know if that's necessary. I can keep an eye on him at home just as well."

He was right. As a medical professional he knew exactly what changes to look for. Still, he was also Danny's father and if she sent Danny home, Quinn would get little if any sleep.

"Yes, you could," she admitted, "but Danny does have a concussion and rather than put the burden on you, I'd prefer to keep him here so that we can keep a close eye out for any subtle neurologic changes. Besides, with that cast he's going to need some decent pain management during the night, too."

When Quinn still hesitated, his expression torn, she put a reassuring hand on his arm. "Stay for one night. By the morning he should be feeling better."

He stared at her hand and then slowly lifted his gaze to her face. Just as before, a strange undercurrent of awareness tingled between them and she saw a flash of desire in his eyes before it vanished so quickly she might have imagined it.

"All right. We'll stay."

"Great." She dropped her hand from his arm, and tried not to cover her confusion. She didn't understand why she reacted this way to a man who was nothing more than a colleague. She turned toward the door. "I'll tell Jadon to arrange for a bed."

"Leila?" His deep husky voice saying her name stopped her in her tracks.

Her mouth went dry. She nervously licked her lips as she turned to face him. "Yes?"

"Thanks." His serious gaze bored into hers. "You were wonderful with Danny."

"You're welcome." She smiled and then went out to the arena to ask Amy to arrange for Danny's transfer upstairs.

Once the task was finished, she went to relax in the lounge, letting Jadon take over the management of the ED. As she let her eyes drift closed, she tried to figure out why loathing Quinn Torres had been so much easier than liking him.

Quinn's forearm tingled from Leila's innocent touch long after she'd left. He took several deep breaths, trying to ignore the sensation, but to no avail. Of course, it didn't help that a hint of her jasmine scent lingered in the air.

Admit it, he told himself harshly, you're sexually attracted to her, no matter how much you wish you weren't. Quinn took a deep breath and let it out slowly. He would have preferred his hormones to stay in their deep freeze rather than flowing hotly, urgently through his bloodstream like heat-seeking missiles aiming for the closest female within touching distance.

He closed his eyes, trying to slow his racing heart, knowing that Delores was probably right. He'd been alone for too long. Thank heavens she wasn't here as he didn't think he'd hidden his reaction to Leila very well and she would have pounced on the attraction with a barely restrained glee.

He wasn't interested in a relationship. Would never again open himself up to the pain and agony of marriage. But he wasn't a monk either. Apparently his body was letting him know that he needed sex.

Leila's image bloomed in his mind, instantly causing his groin to tighten with need.

No. Not Leila. Not anyone here in Cedar Bluff. Small-town secrets were an oxymoron because there simply weren't any. Everyone always knew everyone else's business. He'd been amazed that he'd been able to hide the truth regarding Danny's muteness for as long as he had. Although he suspected it was just a matter of time before someone became curious enough to search through back newspaper articles to discover the truth.

Not Leila. As much as he didn't particularly like the idea, he'd be better off going to Chicago, losing himself in the anonymity of the big-city bar scene. Normally, he wouldn't even entertain the idea, but what choice did he have? Long-term relationships were out of the question, so he'd have to make do with a quick fling, where no one would get hurt. Women seemed attracted to him and he knew he wouldn't have to go home alone if he didn't want to.

"Dr. Torres? Danny's room is ready now." Amy, the cheerful nurse who'd helped minister to Danny's needs, smiled at him. Annoying to realize he didn't feel one iota of desire for her. So much for his theory about re-sponding to any woman within touching distance. What was wrong with him? Why was he so acutely aware of Leila?

"Thanks." He unfolded his lean frame and stood, stretching the kinks out of his neck. Danny didn't like the bright lights, but tolerated the ride upstairs to the fourth-floor children's wing well enough.

"Is there anything else you need before I go?" Amy asked, her smile a tad too bright. He had the sense she was way too curious about Danny.

Maybe she'd be the one to do the Internet search. The knowledge made him tense and scowl. He would do anything to protect his son.

"No," he said bluntly, not caring if he sounded rude. Rudeness helped keep people's curiosity at bay. When she left, he settled into a chair next to Danny's bed. Seconds later, a young pediatric nurse named Elizabeth came in to perform an admission assessment on his son. He dreaded having to explain about Danny's inability to speak all over again, but Amy must have done a good job of handing over care because Elizabeth didn't pry for more information, but kept her questions to Danny easy so he could simply respond with a nod or head-shake.

Danny didn't want the television on, even with the cartoon channel playing his favorite movie, so Quinn sat in the quiet darkness, forcing himself to relax.

Which wouldn't be so difficult if his thoughts wouldn't persist in returning to Leila.

Chicago. Maybe Delores was right about him needing to get out there. He could use the New-Year weekend to go to Chicago. A night of mindless sex would certainly help erase Leila from his mind.

He must have fallen asleep for a while, because all too soon the nurses brought dinner in for Danny. He watched as they did a very comprehensive neuro check, asking him questions that he helped answer through interpreting Danny's sign language.

"Dr. Torres, we have a parent kit here if you're planning to spend the night," Elizabeth offered.

"Thanks." He took the kit containing toothbrush, toothpaste, a comb, etc., and set it aside. His jeans and sweater had been comfortable enough for sledding but now he found them too warm and constrictive in the confines of Danny's room.

After Danny had eaten his dinner, not much but enough to satisfy the nurses, he stood. "I'll be back in a little while, Danny. I'm going to go down to get a pair of scrubs to change into."

Scrubs? Danny signed. *Can I get some, too?*

"Sorry, but they don't have any kids' sizes," he said. "But your hospital pajamas are very similar to scrubs. I'll show you when I get back how close they'll match."

Okay. Danny settled down onto the bed, not seeming to have too much energy.

"Does your head still hurt?" Quinn asked.

Yes, the light makes it worse.

He tried to squelch his concern, knowing the nurses were keeping a close eye on Danny's concussion. Still, he bent over to give Danny a big hug anyway, grateful that the sledding accident hadn't been worse.

"I'll be right back," he promised.

Quinn paused in the hallway outside Danny's room

to tell Elizabeth he'd be gone for a while, before heading down to the OR locker rooms. All the physician staff were given access, scrubs were provided for everyone free of charge. The physician lounge, located in the center space between the male and female locker rooms, was empty.

Finding his size wasn't easy, the scrubs seemed to be either too big or too small. Finally he found what he needed. Feeling much better in the loose-fitting garments, Quinn bundled up his clothes and headed back into the lounge, stopping short when he found Leila sitting on the small sofa with one leg crossed over the other, her face betraying her exhaustion as she gingerly massaged the sole of one bare foot.

"Quinn." She looked surprised and maybe a little embarrassed to see him. "How's Danny?"

"He's fine." Instantly, her scent filled his head. Damn, since when had he been so tuned in to one woman? Then his gaze dropped to her small, dainty foot. He knew the two trauma surgeons took turns being on call, he'd bet she'd been on her feet all weekend. "You need someone to do that for you," he said, indicating the way she'd continued to massage her foot.

A wry smile tugged at her mouth. "You offering?"

He hadn't meant to, but surprised himself by nodding. "Sure." He set his clothes on a nearby chair and knelt beside her chair.

"No. Really. I was just teasing." With her eyes widening in alarm, Leila dropped her foot and frantically searched for her discarded sock and running shoe.

Ignoring her protests, he brushed aside her hands and took her small, bare foot in his hand. Her skin was satiny soft, just like he'd imagined. And her jasmine scent was driving him crazy. "Those weren't the shoes you were wearing earlier," he noted as he gently began to massage the graceful curve of her arch.

"No." She stared at him, her eyes wide as if she didn't find his massage at all comforting. "You'd think I'd learn not to give in to vanity when those heels are hardly comfortable to wear for hours on end."

"You're beautiful no matter what you wear," he murmured. She'd changed from her blouse, skirt and heels into scrubs. He preferred the heels, too, as they did great things for her legs. But not if they made her feet hurt.

He propped her foot on his thigh and smoothed his hand up the muscles of her calf, extending his massage and enjoying the freedom of touching her. She let out a tiny moan, a look of pure bliss etched on her face.

His body responded instantly, growing hard with desire as he thought of other ways, far more pleasurable ways, to use his hands and eventually his mouth to make her moan. Unable to tear his gaze from her face, he reached for her other foot, intent on providing the same treatment there.

Her foot on his thigh moved sideways against his groin and suddenly her eyes flew open, her foot jerking away after it came into contact with the undeniable evidence of his hard arousal.

"I'm fine. Really. Thanks so much for helping me to get rid of that foot cramp. I really hate it when that happens, don't you?" Leila babbled as she avoided his gaze, almost frantic as she felt around for her shoes and socks.

"Leila." He put his hands over hers, forcing her to stop what she was doing to look at him. "You're a beautiful woman, and I reacted like any normal man. I didn't mean to make you uncomfortable."

She shook her head, but her breathing was erratic, her chest rising and falling rapidly, and her pupils were so dilated her eyes almost looked black. Her straight dark hair fell loosely around her shoulders and he wondered if the strands could possibly be as silky soft as her skin. She licked her lips, drawing his attention to her mouth. A mouth he was suddenly desperate to taste. Beneath her thin scrubs he could see her distended nipples.

She was aroused, too. This burning desire he felt was not at all one-sided.

The knowledge was like adding a stick of dynamite to his already smoldering libido.

CHAPTER FOUR

DEAR heaven, Quinn was going to kiss her. Leila read his intention in his dark gaze even before his head dipped toward her.

But she didn't move, didn't back away. Didn't even try to stop him.

Because she wanted him to kiss her.

Eyes wide, she held her breath and watched him close the gap between them. He cupped the side of her face with one large brown hand, the rough calluses sending shivers of awareness dancing across her skin as he smoothly, oh, so smoothly covered her mouth with his.

There was no hesitancy, no gentle pressure in a let's-get-to-know-each-other kind of way. Instead, his mouth was hot and demanding, overwhelming her with barely restrained desire. She was instantly swept away in a blaze of need, hanging on to his broad shoulders and kissing him back with a fierce urgency that was so foreign she didn't recognize herself.

More, she wanted more. She tore at his scrubs, wishing the fabric would disintegrate so she could touch him. She wanted him. Dizzying sensations swirled through her body, clouding her brain in a red-hot haze of passion. Her thoughts were jumbled in her mind, and all she could think about was how much she craved this. Craved him. Within seconds he had her pressed back against the chair, one hand still cradling her head, the other tucked in the small of her back, urging her forward as his large body pressed intimately against her.

The kiss seemed to go on forever, and yet not nearly long enough. The juncture of her thighs was damp, aching with need. She'd never been so aroused by a mere kiss. When he released her mouth to explore the cleavage hidden in the deep V-neck of her scrubs, she stared at the ceiling above. The room slowly came into focus, reminding her of where they were.

What on earth was she doing?

What if someone came in and saw them? She was abruptly, painfully aware of how wanton she must look, with her legs spread wide to accommodate his body pressing against her. Good grief, their scrubs were so thin she could feel every hard inch of him. They were practically naked.

Weakly, she gave his chest a push. He froze, and then slowly lifted his head, his gaze boring into hers, his brows raised questioningly.

"Quinn, don't. Ah, we can't—we can't do this." She forced the words out, although she knew they sounded lame and not very convincing.

His mouth was too close, his musky male scent too intoxicating. If he didn't move soon she was liable to pull him down again, losing herself in another of his spectacular kisses, and to heck with rational logic.

Finally he eased back, giving her a little breathing room, but still on his knees in front of her. His eyes blazed with desire and his voice was deep and husky when he finally spoke.

"Are you married?" he asked.

"What?" Appalled, she gaped at him. Where had that question come from? "No! Of course not. Do you really think this…" she helplessly waved a hand between them "…would have happened if I were *married?*"

A strained smile lifted the corner of his mouth and the transformation was enough to make her suck in a harsh breath. Lord have mercy, he was handsome. She didn't even want to imagine how much more so he'd look with a full-blown, real smile on his face.

Italian. After that kiss, he had to be Italian.

"You're not married and I'm not married but you still want me to stop?" One brow lifted arrogantly, as if he was smugly aware of how incapable she was of turning him down.

Thankfully, his arrogance restored her ability to think. And to act.

"I don't jump into bed with every man who's not married," she said tartly, giving him another shove to put even more distance between them. "Especially not with an unmarried man I don't even *like.*"

He laughed. The arrogant jerk actually had the gall to laugh! White-hot fury simmered behind her eyeballs, helping her ignore his far-too-gorgeous-for-his-own-good looks.

"*Quierda,* if the heat of that kiss was an indication

of how much you dislike me, then I can assure you I don't mind." His eyes—black devil eyes, damn him—practically danced with frank amusement. "You can hate me any time."

That declaration was so ridiculous she wouldn't demean herself by responding. Leila gave him another shove, almost kicking him with her haste to pull her legs together so she could jump to her feet. The more distance between them, the better. She grimaced, feeling absurd when she felt the cold tile beneath her one bare foot.

He'd called her *darling* in Spanish. He had to be from Spain. Italian men were generally not nearly as arrogant as Spaniards.

Gathering her poise and ignoring her one-shoe-off-and-one-shoe-on situation, she crossed her arms over her chest, watching as he slowly rose to his feet, towering over her petite frame by a good twelve to fourteen inches.

She swallowed hard, her gaze clinging to his broad shoulders. Maybe she should have stayed seated. She liked it better when he was on his knees before her.

Stop it. She mentally smacked some sense into her head. What was wrong with her? How could she have gotten herself into this situation? She needed to get rid of Quinn now.

"This interlude is over. I need to get back to work." She pinned him with a haughty glare. "And I'm sure your son is wondering where you are."

"Have dinner with me tomorrow."

Oh, for heaven's sake. Hadn't the obtuse man heard a word she'd said?

"I'll pick you up at seven." He pressed her missing sock into her hand and then bent down to pick up his clothes before walking past her out of the physician lounge. She blinked, staring at the closed door in dismay.

Seven? She hadn't agreed to go out with the conceited oaf.

Had she?

Leila rubbed her burning eyes. Her long weekend of work was over, but no matter how exhausted she was physically she couldn't sleep.

It was all Quinn's fault.

She'd avoided him since their kiss. Which hadn't been difficult as she'd come home late and he was probably still at the hospital with his son. It was difficult to reconcile the man she'd thought him to be with the man she was learning he actually was. Since thinking of kissing Quinn made her heart beat fast and her chest ache with desire, she firmly pushed him from her mind.

She needed something else to think about. Something other than Quinn, because he made her think of sex, which wasn't good. She normally wasn't a sensual woman. She'd never been tempted to partake in a one-night stand, her work had always come first. Not that she'd lived the life of a nun. She'd been happily married to George, a professor at the local university, for two years before he'd died. Maybe their lovemaking hadn't been filled with fiery passion, but it had been satisfying in a sweet, romantic way.

Lust wasn't love. Those breathless moments with

Quinn had certainly proved that. Good grief, she'd never thought she could be so tempted by mere lust.

She wasn't having dinner with him. No way. After she got some decent sleep, she planned to call him and tell him not to bother picking her up. Hopefully he wouldn't be able to find out where she lived, as her number wasn't listed in the phone book.

He could probably get her phone number from the hospital, though. Okay, fine. When he called her to ask for her address, she'd let him know she wasn't interested.

Liar.

Enough thinking about Quinn. Leila climbed out of bed, slipped on a robe and slippers and padded into her small office located in the second bedroom of her compact three-bedroom ranch-style home.

Searching for her birth mother and for key information about her heritage would help her to forget about Quinn. This was the reason she'd decided not to have children of her own. She couldn't tell her child anything about a medical history. Or even an ethnic one.

After logging onto her computer, she went to her list of favorites and clicked on the first link. She checked the reunion Web site, where adopted children could try to link up with their birth parents, but there was no response to her query looking for the woman she sought by the name of Maylyn Aquino.

Her mother's surname came from the Philippines, but that was about all she knew of the woman who'd given birth to her. A name and age. Maylyn had been nineteen when she'd given Leila up for adoption, and she knew nothing at all about her father.

Big blanks in her past that she'd hoped one day to fill with knowledge.

Leila had pored over pictures of Filipino women, looking for similarities matching her facial features, but while there were some resemblances, she'd decided that either her mother had been only part Filipino or her father had diluted the gene pool because she still looked different.

She sighed and pushed away from the computer. Her foster parents had discouraged her from seeking the truth about her heritage, explaining how she should be glad she looked unique.

Leila hadn't been able to make them understand that it was more than just finding out about her heritage. It was about seeking a sense of identity. Of knowing more about her mother's family, the people she'd descended from.

Aquino was a common last name, though, so it was nearly impossible to track down her mother's family. Not without knowing more about Maylyn. When had she come to the U.S.? Or had she been born here? Were her maternal grandparents full-blooded Filipinos or had one of them been Caucasian?

So many questions with so few answers. George hadn't understood her secret need to know about her past, and had discouraged her from seeking information in the same way her foster parents had.

Now George was gone and she'd found herself spending way too much time looking through reunion Web sites and tracing Filipino family histories.

No wonder she didn't have a social life.

With a wide yawn, she realized the time was close

to two in the morning. She really needed to get some sleep. After shutting down the computer, she headed back to bed.

She snuggled under the covers, her mind relaxing. Finally, she'd get some rest.

Before sleep could fully claim her, though, she wondered about Quinn's ethnic background. She'd been second-guessing herself over and over again. Of course she could simply come straight out and ask him.

Unlike her, he likely knew his family roots.

Restless and edgy, Quinn woke early on Monday morning, his dreams far more X-rated than they had a right to be, considering his son was still sleeping off the effects of a concussion in a hospital bed just a few feet away.

He raked a hand over his face, blew out a long breath and debated if he had time for another cold shower. Although the one last night hadn't worked so he wasn't sure why he thought another one would.

Leila had gotten under his skin. Her scent was deeply embedded in his brain. He couldn't stop thinking about her.

If this was the result of two years of dormant hormones, maybe he should have taken Delores's advice and attempted to jump-start them a little sooner.

This reaction couldn't be the result of Leila alone. Surely his mind was simply playing tricks on him. Even Celeste hadn't gotten him so hard so fast.

A knock on Danny's door had him glancing up in surprise. Not Leila, of course, she was probably at home sleeping in after her weekend on call, but Dr. Andrew

Tobin, Danny's pediatrician, the same one that Kylie Germaine used for Ben, came into the room.

"He's still sleeping?" Andrew asked with a slight frown.

"He's been up periodically through the night," Quinn responded. "According to the nurses, his neuro checks have remained stable."

"Hmm." Andrew Tobin approached Danny's bed, gently shaking his shoulder to wake him up. "Danny? It's Dr. Tobin. Can you open your eyes for me?"

His son was used to the routine by now, after having his pupils checked all night. Quinn approached the bed to help with interpreting Danny's sign language.

"Before we send him home, we want to do one more CT scan of his head," Dr. Tobin said, after completing his exam.

"Sounds good." Danny had been in quite a bit of pain from his broken leg through the night as well and they'd been a little cautious about giving pain medication. "If he's clear, does that mean he can have higher doses of pain medication?"

"Sure," Andrew said with a nod.

Satisfied that everything was going well, Quinn accompanied Danny to Radiology and mentally began to plan for his date with Leila. He wanted to take her somewhere elegant yet private. He half expected her to try to call and get out of it, but he wasn't going to accept no for an answer. The sexual chemistry between them was volatile, there was no way they could simply ignore it and hope it would go away.

Going to Chicago would have been smarter, but the thought of leaving Danny for a weekend didn't appeal.

He knew he didn't deserve a relationship, but what if he could find someone who would settle for what he could offer? Sex with no strings attached? Unfortunately, the only woman he could even imagine being with right now was Leila.

What they shared was too strong, too powerful to ignore. He wanted to spend more time with her and if he did, he thought it was likely they'd both give in to what they wanted.

Yet the last thing he wanted to do was to hurt her. Better to make the expectations clear up front, to avoid messy entanglements later.

Once they were back in Danny's room, his cell phone rang. His stomach clenched, but when he glanced at the display, he noted the caller was Delores, who must still be in Chicago.

"Quinn? Where on earth are you and Danny?" she demanded.

He winced a little, realizing that he'd forgotten to call her, even after Danny had reminded him. "Sorry, Delores, but we're at the hospital. Nothing serious," he added quickly when she gasped loudly. "Danny broke his leg in a sledding accident. He also had a mild concussion. He spent the night here, but we just did another CT scan of his head and if it's clear, I'll be bringing him home."

"Broken leg? Concussion? And you didn't call me?" Delores's tone was shrill.

He grimaced and held the phone away from his ear. She had a right to be angry, but did she have to be so loud? "I'm sorry. I swear I meant to call you. I didn't want to ruin your trip."

"Don't you think maybe I would have liked to be there for you and Danny?" she demanded.

"Yes, I think you would have immediately come home, which was exactly what I was trying to avoid." He rubbed the back of his neck. "But I do need your help. Will you watch Danny this evening? I have a dinner date."

"You have a dinner date? With a woman?"

"Well, certainly not with a man," he said with a dry laugh.

"Of course I'll be there. What time? Oh, never mind, I'll come home early so that I can cook Danny's favorite meal. He can eat regular food, can't he?"

"Yes, he's fine. His lower leg is in a cast, and they've given him crutches. I'm sure they'll give me some pain medication to bring home for him."

"The poor boy. Tell him we're having spaghetti, his favorite dinner, tonight."

"I will." He breathed a sigh of relief. His diversion tactic had worked. Delores was so happy he was actually going out that she'd gotten over being angry with him.

Mission accomplished. At least one of them. The second, more difficult task was still to be tackled.

He needed to find Leila's home address.

As he started to make phone calls, he realized it might be more difficult than he'd originally thought. She wasn't listed in the phone book. He'd gotten her number easily enough from the ED physician directory, but he didn't want to call her. Instinctively he knew he'd be better off if he simply showed up at her house by seven.

After making dinner reservations for seven forty-five, just in case he needed to give her some extra time, he began tapping his resources. After a few phone calls, he got in touch with Jadon Reichert.

"Leila's address?" Jadon's voice held suspicion. "Why?"

Quinn suppressed a sigh. "I'm not stalking her or anything, so relax. She lost a bracelet in the ED the other day and I found it. I just want to drop it off for her."

It was a blatant lie, but he thought Leila might not exactly want the whole of Cedar Bluff to know he was taking her to dinner. Not that the news wouldn't travel through town soon enough. Still, he thought she'd prefer the lie to telling Jadon the truth.

"Oh, well. In that case, sure. She lives just a few blocks from me, on Howard Avenue. I think her address is two-ten south Howard. It's a one-story tan house with dark green shutters."

Perfect. "Thanks, Jadon. I'm sure she'll appreciate getting her bracelet back ASAP."

"No problem."

He was still basking in the glow of his success when Andrew Tobin returned. "Danny's head CT is all clear, so you're free to take him home. Here's a prescription for stronger pain medication if you need it."

"Great. Thanks very much." He glanced at Danny, who was watching them with wide eyes. He signed and spoke at the same time. "Did you hear that? You're all better, so we can go home."

I heard. Does this mean I can't go sledding anymore?

"Sorry, no sledding until the cast comes off in six to eight weeks," he said. "But just think of how cool you're going to look with that cast. The girls are going to be all over you."

Danny rolled his eyes. *I don't like girls.*

Quinn grinned. "You will."

No way. Danny's expression was firm. *If I'm stuck at home, can Ben and Charlie come play video games with me?*

"Yes. We'll see if one of them can come over later today for a while, okay?"

Danny nodded and Quinn helped him get dressed, quickly realizing that Danny's pants didn't fit over the bulky cast. He borrowed scissors from a nurse and cut a slit in the bottom of the left leg.

"You might want to invest in a few pairs of sweat-pants or the athletic pants that have zippers along the bottom," she suggested. "They're cheaper than buying new jeans."

Another shopping trip, although he knew Delores would help. On the way home, he explained to Danny how Auntie D. was making his favorite dinner.

Where are you going?

Quinn hesitated, not sure how to explain. He wasn't used to providing his son with details about his dating life.

Up until now, he hadn't had a dating life.

And Quinn really, really didn't want Danny to think he was going to have another mother. Danny was still traumatized by what had happened with Celeste.

"I'm having dinner with a doctor friend of mine." He shot Danny a quick glance. "You don't mind, do you?"

Danny shook his head. *Is she pretty?*

He frowned. How had Danny figured out the doctor friend was a woman? Sometimes he forgot that just because Danny didn't speak, it didn't mean his son didn't have acute hearing. He must have overheard Quinn's conversation with Delores.

"Danny, she's just a friend," he hastened to explain. "Adults have dinner as friends all the time. It's nothing serious, so please don't worry about it."

Danny stared at him for a long moment, and then shrugged. *I'm not worried.*

"Good." Quinn's smile was strained. Because suddenly he was worried enough for the both of them.

CHAPTER FIVE

QUINN arrived promptly on Leila's doorstep at five minutes to seven. The look of stunned surprise on her face when she opened the door would have been comical if not for the fact that she very clearly had not planned to go to dinner with him.

Her casual dress was the first clue. Her obvious surprise the second. Yet even in snug black jeans and a deep purple sweater, she was gorgeous.

"How did you get my address?" she demanded in a rather unwelcoming tone, although she did hold the front door open for him.

He smiled and stepped inside out of the cold weather. "I'll wait if you want to change. If not, you're absolutely fine as you are."

Leila's long dark hair was loose, draping over her shoulders, and he wanted very badly to bury his fingers in the silky dark strands. Her expression was full of annoyance and a touch of chagrin as she crossed her arms over her chest. "This isn't a good idea. I don't want to go out with you."

Her words had the power to shake his confidence, but

he hid the effect by simply cocking a brow. "Which is it? Not a good idea or that you really don't want to go?"

"Stop splitting hairs," she snapped, her temper flashing in her violet eyes. "What difference does it make? No is still no."

Too bad he wasn't taking no for an answer. He glanced around her tidy home, noting the absence of dinner preparations. "Have you eaten dinner already?" he asked.

"Not yet," she admitted.

"Then there's really no reason we can't share a simple meal. Certainly you can't argue about a friendly dinner between two colleagues."

"I doubt your intentions are friendly," she groused, half under her breath.

He fought the urge to smile. She was feisty. He liked that about her. Not just feisty but beautiful, smart, talented and sexy.

Very sexy.

So far, he couldn't come up with a single thing he didn't like about Leila Ross.

"What are you so afraid of?" he asked in a soft voice.

That made her angle her chin, her eyes sharp. "I'm not afraid."

"Good. Because I'd hate to think you'd allow fear to control what you did or didn't do."

She stared at him with a narrowed gaze. "Your inflated ego is amazing."

This time he did laugh. She was just so damn cute. "If you really don't want to go out, I'll cancel our reservations and arrange for a delivery instead. I'm not opposed to dining here in your home."

If anything, her eyes widened farther. Sensing the futility of arguing, she agreed. "Fine. We'll go out for dinner and nothing more. Have a seat and I'll be right back." She spun on her heel and stalked down the hall to her bedroom.

He didn't sit. As he watched her walk away, it took all his willpower and then some to stop himself from following her, picking up their heated embrace and her intoxicating kisses where they'd left off yesterday in the physicians' lounge.

As far as he was concerned, they didn't have to go out to eat. He'd rather they didn't. Staying here in the cozy intimacy of her home made it more likely that he'd be able to steal another kiss or two. Maybe more.

Reining in his impatience wasn't easy. He sensed Leila was, indeed, running away. He didn't fully understand why, but he couldn't seem to make himself back off either.

He wanted her. And despite her cutting words to the contrary, he knew she wanted him, too.

She returned to the living room a few minutes later, looking absolutely stunning in a long-sleeved black knit sweater dress that dipped low over her breasts and happened to be short enough to reach mid-thigh, showcasing an awesome pair of legs.

Damn. He swallowed hard, knocked off balance at the sight. "Breathtaking," he murmured in a low, husky voice that didn't come close to hiding his pure male reaction.

"Thank you." If she noticed the blazing hunger in his gaze she pretended to ignore it as she picked up her purse. Her tone was cool and polite. "I'm ready."

Yes. So was he. More than ready. But not for dinner.

Forcing himself to nod, he held the door open for her, inhaling her exotic scent as she brushed past him into the chilly night.

The cold blast of wintery air didn't come close to dousing the fire raging within. He suspected that a dozen cold showers wouldn't do the trick either. Leila wielded some sort of power over him that he was helpless to resist.

She'd managed to turn the tables on him, gaining the upper hand in this sensual dance. A fact he was afraid she knew only too well.

Yet he couldn't help but smile, because he'd never felt more alive than he did right at that moment.

This was a bad idea. Leila forced herself to breathe through her mouth, because Quinn's scent was filling her head with all sorts of crazy ideas, including finding a way to kiss him again.

A really, really bad idea.

But at the time it had also seemed like the lesser of two evils. Having Quinn stay at her house, calling for takeout, eating in the intimacy of her living room, would have been a worse idea.

But she wasn't afraid of him. Absolutely not. If anything, she was afraid of herself. She didn't trust her own reaction to him. Or her ability to resist him if he focused all that male sexual energy toward her again.

Hysterical laughter bubbled in her throat and she coughed in an effort to pull herself together.

Get a grip. This was only dinner, certainly not a prelude to more kissing or sex. There was no reason they

couldn't simply have a friendly dinner between colleagues.

Sure.

She struggled to stay immune to the sexual heat that
radiated off him, filling the interior of his sports car.
There was no sign of a booster seat, and if she hadn't
seen his son with her own eyes, she'd never believe he
was the father of a six-year-old.

"How's Danny?" she asked, desperate to break the
silence.

He sent her a sideways glance. "Fine. Back to normal
and showing off his cast and crutches to all his friends."

She smiled at the image. "I bet. Knowing Kylie's son
Ben, he's no doubt green with envy. Who's watching
him for you tonight?"

"Delores. Danny calls her Auntie D., mostly because
it was easier to learn in sign language than her full
name."

"Has Danny talked at all?" she asked.

The heavy silence warned her—his son's silence
wasn't a topic Quinn cared to discuss. She supposed she
couldn't blame him. She was about to try to cover her
gaffe when he answered.

"No. But he's seeing Nancy Adams, the speech pathologist, so I'm hopeful he'll break his silent streak
soon."

She wanted to ask more, but couldn't think of a way
to ask that didn't sound like she was just being nosy. "He
looks a lot like you. Is your family from Spain?"

Quinn's white teeth flashed in a rare smile. "My
father is from Spain, but my mother was Italian. A lethal
combination, I've been told. They met and married in

Italy, but I was born here in the States. You have a good eye for ethnicity."

Both Spanish and Italian. A lethal combination, indeed. No wonder his charm was so potent. "Different ethnic backgrounds intrigue me."

"Because you're from a mixed culture as well?" he guessed.

Her smile faded. "Yes. I don't know exactly where my genetic makeup comes from, but I do know I have some Filipino blood in my veins."

"Why don't you know? Won't your mother confide in you?"

"My mother gave me up when I was barely three months old. I don't remember her at all. I grew up in foster care."

He threw her a startled look. "I'm sorry. I didn't realize."

She shrugged, shifting uncomfortably in her seat. She wasn't in the habit of discussing her past with anyone and wasn't sure why she'd blurted it out now. "We all have our secrets, don't we?"

He didn't answer, slowing down to pull into the crowded restaurant parking lot of a very nice place well-known for its luxury dining. Leila was very glad she'd changed clothes.

Jeans, even black ones, would have definitely been out of place here.

Red and green lights covered the roof of the restaurant, and two pine trees flanking the entryway were also decorated with the same red and green lights, creating a festive, holiday atmosphere.

Quinn helped her out of the car, tucking her hand in

the crook of his arm to help her navigate the patches of snow and ice in her high heels. A large Christmas wreath was attached to the front door, the scent of pine reminding her that Christmas had only been a couple of days ago.

There was some sort of holiday party being held in the bar/lounge area, and Leila quickly averted her gaze, hoping she wouldn't run into anyone she knew. Not that she needed to explain why she was having dinner with Quinn, but, still, there was nothing a small town like Cedar Bluff loved more than hot gossip.

And she preferred not to have her name linked with Quinn's. After that kiss in the physicians' lounge, she was determined not to be another notch on this particular Latin lover's bedpost.

He might be a father, but Quinn also seemed to be the type of man who could easily leave a trail of broken-hearted women behind him. He was too damn charismatic.

The maitre d' showed them to their table, a small private table isolated from the rest of the dining room by a large column yet providing a spectacular view overlooking the frosty, white-tipped waves of Lake Michigan.

"This is a beautiful place," she told him. "Thanks for bringing me."

"You're very welcome." Quinn took the wine list from the maitre d'. "Would you like a glass of wine?"

"Sure." One glass wouldn't hurt, would it?

His gaze caught hers across the table. "My favorite is Italian wine of course, but you can choose whatever you'd like for this evening."

She waved a hand. "No, go ahead. My husband always claimed I never had a memory for good wine."

"Your husband?" The words were soft but the intensity of his gaze was fierce.

She lifted her chin, refusing to feel guilty. "They found a brain tumor and he was dead within six months."

"I'm sorry." For a moment she could have sworn there was a flash of empathy in his gaze. "Losing him couldn't have been easy."

"No, it wasn't." Talking about George wasn't something she often did either. "I loved him very much."

He stared at her for a long moment. "How long ago did he pass away?"

"Two years. But I still miss him." It was the truth, she did miss him. Although, if she was honest, she'd admit she hadn't thought as much about George since she'd kissed Quinn. The gentle love they'd shared had been overshadowed by Quinn's passion.

Lust was not love, she reminded herself.

The waiter returned, interrupting the slightly tense silence that had grown between them. Quinn ordered the wine. Then the conversation turned to mundane topics as they both perused the menu.

After they chose their dishes, another awkward silence fell between them. Leila tried to think of a neutral topic of conversation, but her mind went blank.

Why in the world had she agreed to this dinner?

"What made you choose Cedar Bluff Hospital as a place to practice medicine?" she asked, falling back on the respective medical profession. "I'll admit from the very beginning I had you pegged as someone that would have been more at home at a larger, more prestigious one."

"I couldn't care less about the prestige offered by any top medical center." Quinn lifted his glass of wine and took a tentative sip, then nodded to the waiter to pour more. "I came here for Danny."

His simple statement rang with truth, causing a pang of guilt for her initial assessment of his priorities. Clearly, Quinn loved his son.

"Very admirable," she murmured, thinking of how difficult it must be as a single man to raise a son on his own. Especially a mute son. She might never have wanted her own children, but she still enjoyed them. Their innocence. Their unconditional love.

"Not admirable. Practical. I grew up in New York and went to college in Boston. But I like it here. Cedar Bluff is a nice change." His tone was brisk, matter-of-fact, and didn't encourage further discussion. "Leila, are you ready to order?"

"Of course. I'll have the apricot grilled salmon," she told the waiter.

"And I'll have the house specialty prime rib, prepared medium-rare," Quinn said, closing his menu with a snap.

The waiter disappeared, leaving them alone again.

She sneaked a glance at his handsome, chiseled features. His white shirt and black trousers with the charcoal-gray coat looked elegant on him. What was she doing here with a man like Quinn? He dressed as if he posed as a magazine cover model. He was so different from George, and not just because her husband had been a few years older and had preferred the typical professor tweed. They were different in almost every single way.

She stared through the window at the red and green lights reflected on the water. They didn't even have their meal yet. What on earth would they talk about during the next hour? She couldn't begin to imagine.

She was tempted to finish off her wine in one large gulp. "I guess I'm out of practice," she said with a sigh.

"No, it's not that." Quinn reached over to take her hand in his large brown one. His thumb stroked the back of her hand, sending shivers up her arm. "You're thinking too much."

Thinking at all was nearly impossible with him touching her. But she refused to let him distract her. "It's no use, Quinn. This was a very nice gesture, but I think it's rather obvious we don't have anything in common."

"You don't think so?" He tightened his grip on her hand, urging her to meet his gaze. "*Quierda*, you're wrong. We have this in common." He lifted his other hand, displaying the fine tremor. "See what you do to me with a mere look?"

She swallowed hard, trying to tug her hand from his. "There has to be more than this," she whispered.

"Do you feel anything remotely like this with anyone else?" he demanded, his impatience taking the form of arrogance. "Well? Do you?"

Slowly she shook her head.

"It's the same for me," he said, in a low urgent voice. "I haven't felt anything like this for a woman in a long time."

"Just because you're lonely—" she began.

"No." He cut her off abruptly. "This isn't loneliness

and you know it. There is something palpable between us. I don't understand. Why do you insist on pretending this chemistry, this complete awareness we share doesn't exist?"

"Because I don't want it to exist." Irritated, she pulled her hand away, nearly spilling what was left of her wine. She knew it was a mistake to come here with him. He was a man who was far too accustomed to getting his way. "Lust is overrated," she said, wishing at the moment she really believed it.

She knew in her head that lust was an empty feeling, something that would burn away quickly, leaving nothing but regrets behind, but at the moment her traitorous body was trying to convince her otherwise.

"No, Leila, I disagree. Love is the complication neither of us needs. I want you, Leila. Very much. We're two uninvolved, consenting adults and I promise to be discreet." He leaned closer, as if he wanted to reach all the way over to kiss her. "Tell me, what is so wrong with exploring the possibility of an affair?"

CHAPTER SIX

AFFAIR? Leila stared at Quinn, half suspecting he was teasing, testing her reaction. Yet the intensity of his gaze warned her he was dead serious. She snapped her mouth closed, realizing she was gaping at him.

In all her thirty-four years no man had ever offered to have an affair with her.

She couldn't believe it was happening now. And she couldn't believe she was tempted, even for a moment, to drown caution in the lake by taking him up on his ridiculous offer.

"Thanks, but I think I'll pass." *Coward*, the devil on her shoulder hissed.

He merely quirked a brow, tilting his head as if she were some unknown specimen he was curious about. "Would you mind telling me why?"

Why? Wasn't it obvious? She had no idea what had happened to Danny's mother but Quinn's comment about love being a complication led her to believe he didn't miss her, at least not in the same way she missed George. She didn't know if she could have sex with someone without being in a relationship. And a relationship with Quinn would be trouble. A fact she knew with every nerve in her body.

Yet her heart beat rapidly in her chest, betraying her interest in Quinn on a personal level. She did her best to ignore her physical reaction to him. "Because I'm not the sort of woman who jumps heedlessly into an affair." She mentally winced at her prim tone.

Thankfully, the waiter showed up at that moment with their salads. Avoiding Quinn's gaze, she waited as the waiter ground fresh pepper over hers before picking up her fork.

"This looks delicious," she murmured, as if they hadn't been calmly discussing an affair a few moments earlier.

"Absolutely," he agreed, although his eyes weren't on his food. Instead, they seemed to cling to her face. She wished he'd stop staring at her like that.

Deciding she didn't have to speak as long as her mouth was full of food, she dug into her salad, even though she wasn't exactly hungry. Her stomach was knotted up with tension, the same feeling she'd always had around Quinn from the first moment she'd met him.

A few days ago she'd thought he was an arrogant jerk. Now she wasn't sure what to think. He was still arrogant. Arrogant and persistent. Obtuse. Defiantly obtuse.

"Tell me, Leila, exactly what sort of woman does agree to an affair?" he asked between bites. "One who believes sex is immoral?"

She momentarily closed her eyes. Why didn't he just drop the subject? "I never said that."

"Ah, so it's just an affair with me that you object to?"

He continued speaking as if discussing the possibility of having sex was an everyday topic for dinner conversation. "I don't believe you're prejudiced against my mixture of Spanish and Italian blood, since you're not even certain what nationality you are. Maybe it's because of Danny? Do you think I should stop living my life because I'm a single man raising a son?"

"Quinn, please. You must know that's not true either." She swallowed a sigh, trying not to show her rising frustration. "Can't you just accept the fact that we're colleagues and that's all? This was supposed to be a friendly dinner. Stop trying to make it into something more."

He stared at her for a long moment and finally gave a regal nod of his head, agreeing to her wishes. And then, just as smoothly, he asked about where she'd completed her residency program.

Grateful to be back on a safe topic, she found herself relaxing enough to enjoy the rest of the meal as they compared medical school and residency stories. Of course he'd gone to Yale, while she'd attended the University of Madison, but the differences didn't seem so great now that they were both on the staff at Cedar Bluff. By silent, mutual consent, they stayed away from personal topics, like her brief marriage and Danny's muteness.

"Would you care for dessert this evening?" the waiter asked, once he'd cleared away their empty dinner plates.

"No, thank you, I couldn't possibly eat another bite," she said with a satisfied smile.

"Coffee?" Quinn asked.

"Not for me. I'd like to sleep through the night

tonight, after being up most of the weekend," Leila said with a wry grin. "But help yourself."

"I'd better not. Danny likes to be up early." Quinn glanced at the waiter. "I'll take the check, please."

The waiter slipped the bill to him as he finished clearing away their empty wineglasses. Leila wished she could pay for her part of the meal, but suspected Quinn would take offense. Since he'd dropped the heavy seduction act, she decided this was not the time to risk their fragile truce.

Once he'd finished paying for the meal, she stood. Quinn took her arm, leading her back through the crowded restaurant to the coat check. When they stepped outside, he clicked a button on his key fob, remotely starting his car.

"Wow, I need one of those," she murmured.

He chuckled beside her as she gingerly made her way across the slick parking lot. Just as they reached his car, she slipped on an icy patch of snow. With quick reflexes, his arm tightened around her.

"I'm fine," she started to say, but her sentence was cut short when Quinn caught her close and covered her mouth with his.

She put her hand up to push him away, but the heat of his mouth robbed her brain of thought. His tongue probed hers, containing the potency of the Italian wine they'd shared, the effect just as lethal against her defenses.

She didn't notice the cold air around them, because Quinn was so warm. She wound her arms around his neck, thrusting her fingers into his silky black hair as he pulled her closer against his lean, hard frame. His kiss was unrelenting, hot and primitive as his tongue thrust deep, mimicking exactly what he wanted to do.

When he finally lifted his head, she leaned weakly against him, trying to catch her breath. Dear heaven, how could she have let this happen? In the middle of the parking lot, no less?

"I think you're lying to yourself, *quierda*," he whispered in her ear. "An affair is exactly what you need. What we both need. Think about it."

She couldn't answer, had to concentrate enough on maintaining her balance as he stepped away, his hands sliding down her arms, as if he couldn't bear to let her go. She wanted to tell him to go soak his head, but the words were stuck in her throat, congealed by the heat they'd generated. Maybe she needed to stick her head in the nearest snowbank.

Think about it? Thanks to him she doubted she'd be able to think of anything else.

He opened the passenger door and the heated interior reminded her that it was cold. Too cold to stand around contemplating Quinn's kiss.

In silence, Quinn drove her home. She knew she should say something, anything, but her mind refused to function. Quinn didn't seem particularly talkative either.

When they arrived at her house, she wasn't sure if she was glad or disappointed when he left the engine running as he climbed from the driver's seat to walk her to the door.

"Goodnight, Quinn," she managed as he stood, looking down at her.

"Goodnight, Leila. I'll be waiting to hear from you."

He brushed his mouth against hers in a brief kiss, as if to remind her of what she was missing, before he turned and walked back to his car.

Leila fumbled a bit with the key before she managed to get inside her house, closing the door behind her.

She leaned back against the door, listening as Quinn's car backed out of her driveway.

Waiting? For her?

As much as she'd wanted to tartly inform him that he'd be waiting until his hair turned gray and Danny was old enough to attend college, she was very much afraid he was right.

She wanted him. More than she'd ever wanted any other man. Even George.

Especially George.

And, heaven help her, she didn't seem to have the strength to resist Quinn.

Quinn's entire body ached with frustrated sexual tension, robbing him of his ability to sleep.

He should have had the coffee. Should have probably volunteered to work the night shift tonight, since he was wide awake and unable to sleep anyway.

When he closed his eyes, trying to force his muscles to relax, the image of Leila's face shimmered in his mind. Had he pushed too hard? His body vibrated with impatience. No, there was no way he'd imagined her response.

She wanted him, as much as he wanted her. But she was fighting the attraction, trying to resist him. Why, he wasn't certain, although he suspected an underlying fear played a role.

Not fear of him. His eyes shot open at the thought. Could it be? No, she didn't fear him. The way she'd instantly melted in his arms convinced him she wasn't afraid of him. What she feared must be something inside herself.

And somehow he needed to find patience as she took whatever time she needed to figure it out.

Getting out of bed, he padded to the window and stared out at the snow-covered ground as heat radiated off his skin.

Time for another cold shower.

He had a feeling he'd be experiencing plenty of cold showers until Leila was brave enough to come to him.

And what if she didn't come to him? What if she gained strength from being distant from him? The mere thought brought a wave of panic.

Twenty-four hours, he thought grimly, staring blindly at the stark, wintery landscape. He'd give her twenty-four hours. A day that would seem a lifetime.

And then he'd go to her.

"Quinn? Quinn! Wake up, you're upsetting Danny."

He came awake in a rush, squinting at Delores, who stood at the side of his bed, and grabbing the sheets in a reflexive move to make sure his lower body was well covered. Didn't a man get any privacy in his own home? And what was she saying about Danny? "What's wrong? Danny?"

"You wouldn't wake up, that's what's wrong. And Danny thought there was something wrong with you." Delores's tone was full of irritation. "Did you stay up all night?"

Shame chased the rest of his exhaustion away. "Not on purpose," he muttered in response to her question. "Where's Danny? I need to see him."

"Right behind me," Delores said dryly. She turned to Danny, who hovered in the doorway, looking like a waif propped up on his crutches. "See, Danny? I told you your dad was just sleeping."

"I'm sorry, Danny," Quinn said, feeling awful. "I didn't mean to scare you."

His son lifted a shoulder in a casual shrug, but Quinn wasn't fooled. He could still see the remnants of stark terror in Danny's haunted eyes. Quinn gestured for his son to come into the room and Delores left, giving them a few moments alone.

"I'm sorry," Quinn murmured again, drawing Danny close for a big hug. "I'm here. I'll always be here. I won't leave you."

Danny didn't respond, but buried his face against his chest, clinging to his shoulders with a firm grip. Quinn held Danny for a long time, rocking him back and forth, trying to instill a sense of safety and reassurance.

Finally Danny broke away and flashed a small smile. He rested against the bed frame as his fingers flew. *Auntie D. has breakfast ready. She made chocolate-chip pancakes.*

"Sounds good. I'm starved," Quinn said. He wished more than anything he didn't have to work second shift later that day. He felt bad about unintentionally scaring Danny. "Let's go. We have some time to play some video games after breakfast."

You have to work today? Danny asked, his brow puckered.

"I'm afraid so." Quinn captured his son's gaze and deliberately held it. "If you would rather I stay home with you, I'll try to find someone to cover my shift." It was a Tuesday night, shouldn't be that difficult to find cover.

There was a long pause, but then Danny shook his head, his fingers nimble as he signed, *No, there's no reason for you to stay home. I'm fine.*

"Are you sure?" Quinn asked. "Because nothing in the whole world is more important to me than you, Danny. *Nothing.*"

Not even Leila, and it was time he figured that out. Sex was sex but Danny was his life.

I'm sure. I love you, Dad.

"I love you, too." Quinn gave his son another quick, hard hug and then grabbed his robe to follow Danny into the kitchen.

"There you are," Delores said by way of greeting. "Hurry up and eat before the pancakes get cold."

"Yes, ma'am," Quinn said. He caught Danny's gaze and sent him a secret wink behind Delores's back. Danny giggled, but then clapped a hand over his mouth in a belated effort to hide it.

He decided then and there to spend the day with his son, at least until three o'clock that afternoon as that was the time he was scheduled to work.

Leila wasn't a part of his life, at least not this part. He glanced around the small, homey kitchen with satisfaction. He, Danny and Delores were a family. They'd come a long way over the past eighteen months from the broken family they'd been when Celeste had died.

Leila had distracted him in a big way. And he

couldn't afford to let her become so much of a distraction that she had a negative impact on his relationship with his son.

Leila walked through the ICU at Cedar Bluff, checking out her patients from the weekend. Luckily, Jimmy, the young man with appendicitis, had been transferred out of the ICU to a general floor bed, so he was clearly headed in the right direction.

She only had two days on call this week, partially because she'd been on call during the entire weekend. And she was off for New Year's Eve, which was also nice, not that she had any specific plans other than maybe going to Seth and Kylie's wedding.

Would Quinn go, too? Her heart gave a betraying thump and she told herself not to get too excited. She hadn't even made up her mind yet about seeing Quinn again.

I'll be waiting for you.

She shook off thoughts of Quinn to concentrate on her patients. There was another multiple trauma case, a young woman who'd been involved in a snowmobile crash and was still in the ICU. Leila discussed the young woman's care with the critical care intensivist on duty, Dr. Rand Geary, who'd agreed to her suggestion of trying a new medication regimen to get the patient weaned off the ventilator.

Satisfied things were progressing as well as could be expected, Leila finished her rounds in the ICU and then headed out to the floor. She stopped in Jimmy's room last, informing him and his parents that he was doing well enough to be discharged home.

They thanked her profusely and it was times like this when she really enjoyed her job, knowing that she'd helped make a difference in someone's life. She hadn't been able to save Anton, but she had saved many others.

She preferred to focus on the positive side of the win-loss columns. The losses could pull you into a never-ending pit of despair.

Just after dinner, her pager went off, announcing two victims of a motor vehicle crash, one adult and one child, estimated to be about eight or nine.

Her stomach clenched in warning. Children were always the hardest. Another reason she'd been glad she'd decided not to have any. The image of Danny's young face bloomed in her mind.

Bypassing the elevators, she took the stairs down to the emergency department, coming to an abrupt halt when she saw Quinn standing in the middle of the trauma room as the staff hurried to prepare for the new arrivals. Ridiculous to be nervous just because he'd kissed her. And because she'd let him kiss her.

Not just once but twice. Three times, if you counted that goodnight kiss. Which she didn't.

He glanced at her and nodded in greeting. "Two victims of a motor vehicle crash, a father and his son. Hit a light pole going at a high rate of speed. Prolonged extrication at the scene for the adult."

So he was going to keep things professional, which was good as he'd promised to be discreet. And a man interested in an affair wouldn't necessarily ask for more than she could give. Not that she'd agreed to have an affair with him.

Yet.

She hid her flash of disappointment. This was exactly what she'd wanted, right? She glanced around the empty trauma room. "Why haven't they brought the child in yet?"

"He's on his way." The words were barely out of Quinn's mouth when the doors from the ambulance bay burst open, revealing paramedic personnel surrounding a small patient nearly lost in the equipment around the stretcher.

She stood back, watching Quinn take control of the situation. As a trauma surgeon she often assisted with trauma resuscitations but the ED physician was always the one in charge. Her role was mainly that of a consultant, up until the point that surgery was deemed necessary.

Then the patient became hers.

Quinn was impressive, giving orders in a calm, reasonable tone. The boy's injuries didn't appear as bad as she'd feared. Luckily he'd been saved in part by wearing a seat belt and by the passenger-seat air bag.

"Once he's stabilized I'd like a complete head-to-toe CT scan," she told Quinn. "I need to make sure he's not bleeding internally."

Quinn nodded, barely sparing her a glance. They'd pretty much taken care of the child when the double doors of the ambulance bay opened again, bringing in the adult victim.

Easy to see the adult, a male in his late thirties, had taken the brunt of the crash. The odor of alcohol emanating from him was overwhelming.

Quinn's voice took on a frosty edge. "Get a baseline set of labs, including a drug and alcohol screen."

Her brows rose. That wasn't usually the first lab order to get on a multiple trauma patient, but she thought she understood Quinn's frustration. No doubt the eight-year-old victim had reminded him of Danny.

And this man, the father, had nearly killed his son by driving under the influence of alcohol.

CHAPTER SEVEN

"VITALS?" Quinn asked, as soon as the nurse had drawn the necessary labs. In addition to the toxicology screen, Quinn had ordered the standard electrolyte panel and hemotology workup. Leila let Quinn take the lead on the trauma resuscitation, allowing him to get Carl Wolsky, the father of the eight-year-old victim, stabilized before she stepped in to evaluate him for surgery.

"Blood pressure is low, eighty-eight over forty-two."

"Make sure you let me know what his hemoglobin and hematocrit is as soon as you get the results," Quinn said. "He looks as if he sustained chest trauma from the air bag."

Chest trauma meant possible surgery. She wasn't surprised, considering the long extrication at the scene. Leila inched forward, checking to see if Carl showed signs of a flail chest. "I'd like to evaluate him when he's stable enough."

Quinn nodded, although his expression remained tense, his tone clipped with anger as he barked out orders. "I want a portable chest X-ray, stat. Do you have the urinary catheter placed yet? I need to know what his urine output is. And I want to know those lab results as soon as possible."

"Including the drug and alcohol screen?" one of the nurses muttered sarcastically under her breath.

Leila winced, expecting a sharp response, but luckily Quinn ignored her.

"Dr. Ross?" Amy, one of the trauma nurses, came up beside her. "I think you'd better take another look at Trevor, the eight-year-old. He's in a lot of pain and his abdomen has grown firm and tense."

Alarmed, she nodded and quickly hurried over to the first patient, Trevor Wolsky. They'd stabilized the boy initially and had then ordered the total body CT scan. While he'd been undergoing the procedure, they'd turned their attention to Trevor's father.

The youngster's facial expression reflected pain but as he was on a ventilator he couldn't talk. They'd given him a touch of pain medication earlier, but he obviously needed more. "Give him a milligram of morphine," she ordered, as she stepped up to gently palpate the boy's tense abdomen.

His expression got worse the moment she touched him. Definitely not good.

"Dr. Ross? Radiology is on line one for you."

"Thanks." She crossed over to the nearest phone. "Have you read Trevor Wolsky's CT scan yet?"

"Yes, he has a large hematoma forming around his liver. There's also a questionable area of bleeding around his spleen but it's not as large as the liver laceration. His brain and his kidneys are clear."

"All right. Thanks for letting me know." Leila hung up the phone, realizing she'd need to get Trevor to the

OR to explore his abdomen. "Amy, do you know if Trevor's mother has been contacted? He's going to need to go to the OR and if possible I'd like her consent before we go."

"I think the social worker was trying to get in touch with her," Amy said. "I'll find out and let you know."

Leila walked back over to Quinn, who was wearing a sterile gown and in the process of inserting a chest tube into the boy's father. "Bleeding into his chest?" she guessed.

"Yes. I'm afraid he's going to need a trip to the OR for a thoracotomy," Quinn said from behind his sterile face mask. Sure enough, the moment he placed the chest tube, blood began pouring out at a brisk rate.

Leila's heart sank. They weren't a level-one trauma center, they only had two trauma surgeons on staff. It wasn't as if she could call someone else in to help. They could send the patient elsewhere but that might take time, too, considering the bad weather. Of course, they were having the snowiest winter on record. "His son, Trevor, needs surgery, too. But it looks as if the father's injuries are more severe. I should probably take him first."

"No." There was a moment of stunned silence as she stared at Quinn in surprise. "I can auto-transfuse this blood from his chest tube back into him while you finish up with Trevor," he added slowly.

Her eyes widened at his implication. "You're saying you want me to take Trevor to the OR first?"

Quinn nodded. "Children have a higher risk of dying from internal bleeding than an adult. He should go first.

I can safely manage the father, keeping him stabilized, while you operate on his son."

She hesitated, not necessarily agreeing with Quinn's logic. Internal chest bleeding was usually a higher priority than a hematoma in the abdomen, but he was right—children were more susceptible to complications. Still, she couldn't help thinking that the real reason Quinn wanted her to take the child first was because he didn't think Trevor's father was worthy enough. After all, the father had caused the boy's injuries.

Yet standing around indecisively wasn't helping either of them, so she nodded quickly. "Okay, I'll explore Trevor's abdomen first. But the moment I'm finished, I want Carl prepped in the OR, ready to go."

"Agreed." Quinn's eyes held relief.

She spun away, catching Amy's gaze. "Let's get Trevor up to the OR, stat."

"I've already called the OR team," Amy acknowledged. "They're expecting us."

"Any word on his mother?" Leila asked.

"No, I'm afraid not. The social worker hasn't gotten in touch with her yet."

Maybe it was for the best, they didn't really have much time to waste. As it was, Leila couldn't help second-guessing herself as she headed up to the OR suites. Trevor did have bleeding around his liver. He did need surgery, just like his father.

As she scrubbed at the sink, prior to entering the OR, she found herself praying that Quinn would keep Carl alive long enough that she could have a good shot at saving both of them.

* * *

Sweat trickled down the back of Quinn's spine as he continued to run the trauma resuscitation. He firmly believed in his heart that Carl would want them to save his son first. After all, he would do the same for Danny without a moment's hesitation. But at the same time he knew that Carl's condition was probably a little more tenuous than he'd led Leila to believe.

"Get the level-one fluid warmer going," he said to the nurse, Melanie. She was relatively new but she'd gotten much more confident during the past two weeks, since they'd seen more than the usual amount of trauma patients. "I want two units of blood and two units of fresh frozen plasma given ASAP."

"Got it." Melanie hurried to do what he'd ordered. He'd also requested that the auto-transfusion chest tube be set up, and Amy, the nurse who'd been taking care of Trevor, had come over to assist once they'd taken the child upstairs to surgery.

The device was working fairly well, but at a much slower pace than he'd liked. Which was why he'd ordered more blood to be given through the rapid infuser.

How much time would Leila need with the boy? An hour? Two? He didn't want her to rush things with Trevor, but he also wouldn't have many options if another trauma patient was brought in. Their team was stretched as it was, considering it was the week between the holidays.

"We're not going to lose him," Quinn muttered, as if trying to convince himself of that fact. "Amy, check another hematocrit and hemoglobin the moment those blood products have been given."

She nodded. "He's still pretty tachy," she observed.

Right. As if she needed to tell him. Quinn could easily see the monitor readings for himself. Patients who were either dehydrated or volume depleted were usually tachycardic. Carl's heart rate had been hovering in the 140s to 150s during the entire resuscitation. Of course, alcohol caused dehydration, too, so they'd been fighting an uphill battle from the start. The patient was both dehydrated and volume depleted from the bleeding.

"Give another two liters of normal saline." Carl's urine had a pink tinge to it, indicating he might have internal bleeding in his kidneys as well as his chest. If his belly became tense and distended, they'd be in real trouble.

Three strikes and you're out.

Hurry up, Leila.

"Dr. Torres? We finally got in touch with Josephine Wolsky, the patient's ex-wife and Trevor's mother. She's on her way in now," Amy informed him.

Great, Quinn thought with a sigh. He would get to be the lucky one to tell the poor woman that her drunken ex-husband, whose blood alcohol level had been double the legal limit, had almost killed their son.

He was confident Leila would pull the boy through surgery. Trevor would be just fine.

"Let me know when she arrives." Quinn didn't take his eyes off Carl's monitor. They weren't gaining much ground with his blood pressure, not even with all the blood and fluid they'd given. "Amy? Any word on those labs?"

"I'll check." She crossed over to the nearest phone.

Within seconds she was back. "Hemoglobin of 7.5 and hematocrit of 20. He's only gained two points on each."

Bad news. With all the blood they'd given to him, he should be up at least six points. "Give four more units of blood and two more units of fresh frozen. We need to get his bleeding under control."

"Do you think it might help to check his coags? If he's a drinker, his liver may not be functioning well to start with," Melanie suggested.

"Good point. Send the coag panel." His gaze narrowed on the heart monitor above Carl's bed. "Has his rhythm changed?"

"Yes, I think it has." Amy went over to the monitor and pressed a button to run a rhythm strip. "His ST segments might be slightly depressed."

"Get a twelve-lead ECG." Quinn hoped Amy was wrong, because if this guy had suffered a myocardial infarction, he was really out of luck. His chances of surviving surgery were growing slimmer by the minute. Quinn glanced at his watch. Nearly forty minutes had passed. Not nearly enough time for Leila to have finished with Trevor.

And if she didn't hurry, it would be too late for Carl.

Leila extracted the hematoma from around Trevor's liver, checking his spleen carefully to make sure there weren't any hidden bleeders. Once she was satisfied there was no more bleeding, she washed out the entire abdominal cavity thoroughly with an antibiotic solution to minimize the risk of infection.

She began the process of closing Trevor's abdomen,

feeling good about the procedure. There was no reason the boy shouldn't recover fully from his injuries.

"Call down to the ED," she told the circulating nurse once she'd closed the muscle. "Let Dr. Torres know I'm ready for him to bring up the next surgical case, the boy's father."

"Will do." The circulating nurse went to the phone hanging on the wall to make the call.

"Dr. Ross?" the nurse called. "Dr. Torres wants to talk to you."

"I can't. I'm not finished closing." She didn't take her attention away from the task at hand. "I'll talk to him when I'm finished here."

The nurse relayed her message. Then she said, "Dr. Torres wants you to know the father has EKG changes, indicating a possible MI."

Damn. Damn! How on earth was she going to successfully operate on a man who was already having an acute myocardial infarct? Yet what choice did they have? His heart attack was likely a result of the powerful air bag deployment, and if she didn't fix the bleeding, his cardiac status would only get worse. With the way he was bleeding, they couldn't afford to send him for a cardiac catheterization first.

"Bring him up anyway," she said. "And hurry. I'm almost finished."

She'd felt good about the positive outcome of Trevor's surgery, but as she stripped off her sterile gown and gloves and headed back to the sinks to scrub up again, she tried not to think about how Carl might not have suffered the MI if she'd taken him to the OR first.

There was nothing she could do to reverse her decision now. All she could do was continue on the path she'd taken, providing the best possible care to Carl once he arrived from the ED.

And live with the consequences of her decision if he died.

Leila swept off her sterile garb and tossed it into the laundry bin, her knees feeling weak. She was exhausted. It had taken three grueling hours, but she'd managed to repair all of Carl Wolsky's traumatic injuries. Because he was still in critical condition, she'd sent him to the ICU.

He was alive and relatively stable at the moment, although she couldn't be certain he'd make it through the rest of the night. Especially if his heart injury didn't get any better. The first thing she'd do would be to contact the cardiologist on call to get his opinion.

After heading into the women's locker room, she changed her scrubs, and then drew on her lab coat. She needed to head into the ICU to check on Carl to make sure the intensivist and the cardiologist had been in to examine him, but she took a moment to pull herself together, sitting down on the small sofa and closing her eyes.

It was a toss-up which ached worse, her head or her feet. Spending hours in the OR tended to be a strain on her body in more ways than one. With a sigh she rested her head back against the cushion, trying to ease the tense muscles of her neck.

The last time she'd been in this lounge, Quinn had kissed her. She wondered where he was now. Still down in the ED? Maybe. She'd lost track of time, but she knew it was late. The second shift in the ED was normally over at eleven o'clock.

At the rate she was going, she might end up spending the night there. Depending on how well Carl did postoperatively. And depending on what the cardiologist's opinion was regarding his myocardial infarction.

She wasn't an open-heart surgeon, the lung surgery she'd done on Carl was about as close as she got to operating on the heart. She could do some chest procedures but they didn't have a heart bypass machine. If Carl needed open-heart surgery, he'd be transferred to Trinity Medical Center in Milwaukee.

After her five-minute break, she stood and walked out of the lounge, taking the elevator to the ICU. Carl Wolsky's room was still full of personnel—two nurses, an ICU tech and the anesthesiologist from the OR, along with the intensivist on duty.

She stood in the doorway for a moment, watching Carl's vitals on the heart monitor. He wasn't doing too badly, considering everything he'd been through.

"Wean him off his vasopressors if his blood pressure stays above one hundred systolic," she told them.

"Dr. Ross, his ex-wife is downstairs in the family center. She's waiting to talk to you."

So they had finally gotten a hold of Trevor's mother. "Okay, I'll go talk to her after I check on Trevor's condition."

"He's doing very well," Carrie, one of the ICU nurses, said. "We've been checking on him, too."

She smiled, understanding the nurse's concern. Between the father and son, they were treating a family. She went down to the pod of ICU beds they used for pediatrics, located on the other side of the room from the adult side, and found Trevor. He did look great. No fever, vitals stable, and breathing comfortably on the vent.

They could probably wean him off the ventilator in the morning, but for now his young body was still under the effects of anethesia. After writing a follow-up note in his chart, she went down to the family center to find Mrs. Wolsky.

Leila found her right away. She'd obviously been crying, and yet she jumped to her feet the moment Leila walked in. "Dr. Ross?"

"Yes, I'm Dr. Ross. Your son Trevor is doing great, we're hoping to get that breathing tube out in the morning. I've also just completed surgery on your husband, Carl. He's still very critical. His heart may have suffered a little damage, but he's stable at the moment."

"That's good news about Trevor. Carl, well, it's good news about him, too, I guess, but we're divorced now. For almost six months."

Leila wasn't too surprised. "I understand. Is there someone else we should contact for Carl?"

"He's not married or seeing anyone that I know of. I've called his mother, she's heading down from Minneapolis." Mrs. Wolsky sniffled loudly and blew her nose in a crumpled tissue. "Is it true? Dr. Torres told me that Carl's alcohol level was twice the legal limit."

What? Why on earth had Quinn told her about Carl's alcohol level? That was confidential information, even if the woman was the patient's wife, which she wasn't! Although, the boy's injuries were significant enough to warrant potential legal action, she still thought Quinn had stepped over the line, big-time. "I'm sorry, but I can't give you that information. You'll need to get what you need from the police report."

The woman's eyes filled with tears. "Don't you care about Trevor? I share joint custody with Carl, but he almost killed our son!"

"I'm sorry," Leila said helplessly. She understood this woman's pain, but her hands were tied. And Quinn shouldn't have told her about the blood alcohol level either. "I know this is a difficult time for you. But Trevor is doing fine. Carl might not be so lucky. Count your blessings for now and worry about the rest later."

Trevor's mother nodded and blew her nose again. Leila made sure she didn't have any other questions before she left.

But she didn't go back up to the ICU. Instead, she marched straight down to the ED, looking for Quinn.

The man had some explaining to do.

CHAPTER EIGHT

QUINN finished writing the admission orders on his last patient, the final task he'd needed to complete before he could go home. Jadon had come in and had been immediately sidetracked by a patient who'd shown up in the midst of a heart attack, which had meant Quinn had to finish the dispositions of the few patients remaining in the arena.

Not that he minded. Heck, since it had been a long evening, the hour a few minutes past eleven-thirty, Quinn figured things could have been worse. He was getting off his shift early for a change.

Just as he left the arena, though, to head to the lounge for his coat, Leila arrived, approaching him with a determined stride. "Quinn, I need to talk to you."

Normally he would have been thrilled at having Leila come and find him, but the glint of fury in her eyes warned him he wasn't going to like this. "What's wrong?"

She steered him into the staff lounge, closing the door behind her with a loud click. "I just finished speaking to Josephine Wolsky, that's what's wrong. What in the world were you thinking?"

He wasn't in the mood for this. He was tired and he wanted to go home. Trevor's tiny bruised face still haunted him, although he'd called earlier up to the ICU and the nurse had told him the boy was doing fine. "I don't know what you're talking about."

"Don't play stupid with me, Quinn. You told her what Carl's blood alcohol level was," she accused, her hands planted on her slim hips. "You broke every privacy rule there is by giving her confidential patient information!"

"Oh, really? I broke the rules? What rights does eight-year-old Trevor have, huh?" He couldn't believe she was so upset. "Who's looking out for his best interests? Certainly not his father. As Trevor's legal guardian, I believe his mother had a right to know the truth." She didn't, according to the letter of the law, but Quinn didn't care. Given the same set of circumstances, he would do the same thing again.

"She has joint custody with Carl," Leila said stubbornly. "The boy's father has rights, too."

"Does that mean he had the right to drive under the influence with his child in the car?" Quinn asked harshly. "I don't think so. Parents are supposed to protect their children from harm. They're not supposed to be selfish, doing whatever the hell they want without thinking about the consequences of their reckless actions!"

Her eyes widened at his vehement tone. And for once she didn't have a snappy comeback.

He blew out a long breath trying to rein in his temper. Trevor's situation had reminded him too much of Celeste and Danny. Physically, Trevor would probably recover from his injuries, but what about emotionally? From Danny, he knew only too well that emotional wounds healed much more slowly than physical ones.

If they healed at all.

Exhausted from the emotional effects of his shift, Quinn abruptly dropped into a chair and cradled his head in his hands. Maybe he had crossed the line with Trevor's case. But only in an attempt to help an eight-year-old boy who never should have been in the car with his intoxicated father in the first place.

He felt Leila sink down beside him, her hand soft and gentle on his shoulder. She kneaded the tense muscles of his shoulders, offering wordless comfort.

The action drained the rest of his anger. With a resigned sigh, he lifted his gaze to hers. "You're right. I should have kept the information about Carl's alcohol level confidential, encouraging Trevor's mother to get a copy of the police report to get the information she needed. I'm certain the district attorney will press charges against the guy." Slowly he shook his head. "I don't know why I told her, other than the fact I was just so angry."

"I know." Leila's voice was soft. "I understand."

He knew she assumed he was relating Trevor's situation to Danny, but Leila didn't know the whole sordid story.

But his past couldn't remain hidden forever. It was only a matter of time.

Leila kept her hand on his shoulder, leaning closer to him. He inhaled her sweet scent, letting the warmth fill his head. Just being with her made him feel better.

And she had to be more exhausted than he was. He'd heard she'd been in the OR with Carl for hours.

Reaching up, he covered her small yet skilled surgeon's hand with his. In a heartbeat the slight touch changed, shimmering with tension.

He turned toward her, pinning her with his gaze as he slid his hand up her slender arm until he could gently cup her face. She didn't move away.

Her mouth was so close, he couldn't help himself. He needed to kiss her more than he needed to eat, sleep or breathe. How could he crave something as simple as a kiss? How was it that he couldn't seem to stay away from this woman?

Sex, he reminded himself, masterfully taking possession of her mouth and reveling in her response as her fingers tightened in his shirt. This was only about sex.

He couldn't allow it to feel like something more.

The door to the lounge opened and then shut again. Just as quickly as whoever had walked in, they'd decided they'd better leave the entwined pair alone.

Regretfully, he lifted his head, pulling oxygen into his lungs with a deep breath, realizing this wasn't the time or the place for this.

"Quinn," she whispered. He loved the way she said his name. She was so beautiful, she made his heart ache.

"Just say the word and I'll take you home." His voice was hoarse with need. It was a rash promise, but he didn't care. He wanted her. Danny was home, sleeping. There was plenty of time to get home before Danny was likely to get up.

No matter what, he was determined to be home in the morning when Danny woke up.

"I can't. Carl's condition is tenuous. I need to stay here tonight."

The stark regret in her eyes helped soothe his ego. He understood there would be times, like now, when patient care had to come first.

Heck, his son would *always* come first.

Reluctantly he nodded and took a step back, putting a bit of space between them. Not that the action helped take the edge off his need. "All right. Hopefully, I'll see you tomorrow."

"Are you working tomorrow, Wednesday?" she asked.

"Yes. Are you on call?"

"No. Not until Thursday."

Great. Their schedules were completely opposite, which would make their ability to find time alone that much more difficult. "Call me," he said in a low, urgent tone. "We'll figure something out."

"All right."

Trying to be satisfied with at least her acknowledgment that they'd see each other again soon, he turned to leave. But then he couldn't help glancing back at her over his shoulder. Her scrubs were slightly askew, her hair tumbling around her shoulders in a silken cloud, having come loose from the rubber band sometime during their kiss.

Walking through the doorway and continuing through to the employee parking lot outside took every ounce of willpower he possessed.

The next morning, Quinn woke up early so that he wouldn't scare Danny again by sleeping too soundly.

Despite the fact that the kids were on winter break from school, his son still tended to rise early.

Danny ran into his room at seven sharp and this time Quinn was ready. He opened one eye and levered himself up on his elbow before Danny managed to reach the bed. Of course, Danny moved a lot more slowly on crutches than he did with two good legs.

"How is your leg feeling?" Quinn asked.

Good. It doesn't hurt anymore. What's for breakfast?

Food. His son was always interested in food. He grinned. "I don't know. Is Auntie D. up yet?"

I didn't see her, Danny signed.

Hmm. Odd, since Delores usually made it a habit to be up earlier than Danny. Quinn hid a yawn and swung his legs out of bed. If Delores wasn't up yet, he needed to make coffee. Fast.

"All right, let's go find something to eat," he told Danny. "I'll make some bacon and eggs."

Danny's eyes widened in surprise. *Auntie D. is going to be mad. She says that stuff is going to clog your arteries.*

In his opinion, Auntie D. read too many health magazines. "She can't be mad if she's the one who overslept," Quinn pointed out.

Danny's cocky grin boosted his mood. They headed into the kitchen, two conspirators in search of real man-food.

Coffee was the first order of business, but as Quinn was frying up the bacon, Delores came out of her bedroom. "Good morning," she said in a strained tone, completely oblivious to their sacrilegious breakfast fare.

"Good morning." Quinn frowned. "What's wrong? You look like you haven't slept much."

"I've been sick to my stomach half the night," she confessed. Delores sat down hard in a chair at the kitchen table, as if her legs had refused to support her. "I don't know what's wrong with me."

Alarmed, he crossed over to her. "Do you have a fever?"

"Not according to the thermometer," she murmured, closing her eyes. "But my whole body aches and the nausea is nonstop."

Quinn tried to hide the extent of his concern. Delores could simply have flu. Yet as much as she insisted on eating healthily, she was in her early sixties. Maybe this was a prelude to a heart condition? "When's the last time you've seen a doctor?" he asked.

She winced a little. "Close to eighteen months. I'm a bit overdue."

It had been eighteen months since Celeste had died. She'd put off going to the doctor because of him and Danny. "Not anymore. You're going in today," Quinn said firmly. "I'll take you myself."

"Nonsense. All this fuss for a touch of flu." Her voice did seem stronger. "Finish making breakfast. I'll be fine."

Quinn glanced at his son, who was watching the adults with wide eyes. Since he knew Danny was hungry, he would finish breakfast first. But Delores was going in to see someone today, whether she liked it or not.

"Danny, come over here and help me with the toast," Quinn said, distracting his son with the task. "Delores, would you like to try some toast? It might settle your stomach."

"Sure," she said gamely, although the expression on her face was one of hesitation.

"Danny, will you make five pieces of toast?" he asked.

Yes. Danny nodded. He used the step stool to reach the toaster on the counter, propping his crutches nearby. Quinn continued to chat as they worked, Danny interjecting with the occasional sign language question, but Quinn knew his son was still worried about Delores.

He was concerned, too.

She seemed better after she'd eaten some toast. Quinn relaxed a bit as he and Danny finished breakfast and then took care of cleaning up the dishes as well. But it was only about an hour later when he heard Delores being sick again in the bathroom.

Danny was playing video games in the living room, so Quinn knocked softly on the door. "Delores? Are you all right?"

There was a long silence before she finally answered the door, looking pale and shaky. "I don't think so," she admitted.

"That's it," he decided. "I'm taking you to the ED now."

She didn't argue and that was nearly as alarming as listening to her being sick.

Quinn tried to hide the extent of his concern from his son. "Hey, Danny, get your hat and coat. We're going to take Auntie D. to see the doctor so she can get some medicine for her tummyache."

Okay. Danny readily abandoned his video-game controls to hunt for his outerwear.

Quinn knew he could have called for an ambulance, but Delores wasn't that badly off and his house was only five minutes from the hospital. They'd be there quicker than it would take for the ambulance to get dispatched. He helped Delores with her coat and then bundled Danny, his crutches and Delores into the car.

At the hospital, he took Danny inside with Delores, because he didn't have much of a choice. The staff immediately put Delores on a heart monitor and drew some blood to check her electrolytes. Shortly thereafter, Seth pulled Quinn aside.

"Her heart is throwing some premature beats, so we're going to work her up for an MI. We've called the cardiologist, just in case."

Damn, Delores's illness was more serious than he'd thought. He'd shrugged off her symptoms as flu but he should have insisted on bringing her in right away. "All right, keep me posted." He walked back into her room to fetch Danny, anxious to protect his son from the seriousness of his aunt's illness. "Come on, let's take a little walk. I'll show you where I work."

Cool.

He took Danny through the main arena, introducing him to some of the staff, and then took him into the staff lounge area, thinking there had to be something back there to help keep the boy occupied for a while. There were snacks, of course, the ED staff always had snacks, but he finally unearthed a deck of playing cards and showed Danny how to play solitaire the old-fashioned way, rather than on the computer.

"Dr. Torres?" Susan poked her head into the staff lounge about fifteen minutes later. "Dr. Taylor wants to talk to you."

"Stay here for a few minutes, Danny, all right? I'll be back shortly."

Danny nodded, his attention on the game.

Quinn hurried to find Seth. "What's wrong?"

"Well, the good news is that so far Delores's cardiac enzymes and her troponin level aren't too high. We've given her a little fluid and she's been feeling better. But given her age and risk factors, the cardiologist would still like to do a cardiac catheterization, just in case."

"Has she agreed to the procedure?" Quinn asked.

Seth grimaced. "No. We could use your help with that. Michael Hendricks, the cardiologist, tried to get her consent but she refused."

"I'll see what I can do to convince her," Quinn said, knowing the woman could be pigheaded and stubborn. He pasted a smile on his face as he entered her room. "I hear you're feeling better."

"Well enough to go home." The spark was back in her eyes. "I guess I was dehydrated, my electrolytes had gotten out of whack. Tell them to let me go home."

"Don't be too hasty," Quinn chided. He knew IV fluids would make her feel better, but right now flu was the least of her concerns. "Your heart put out a few irregular beats, and they'd like to do a procedure just to be sure you're all right."

"I don't need a procedure."

"Delores, you were sick half the night. It might be a sign that something is wrong with your heart. What if you get sick again and I'm not there to help with Danny?

Then what? Are you willing to put Danny through that again?"

The argument was enough to make her snap her mouth shut. After a long moment, she sighed. "Do you really think this heart procedure is necessary?"

Quinn didn't hesitate. "Yes. I do."

"Then I'll have it done."

"Good. Danny and I can wait here for you."

"There's no need to wait," she immediately protested. "I'm sure they'll call you when I'm finished."

He wasn't going to argue about that, either. They'd wait, even if he had to fudge the truth. "All right, then, we'll see you when you're finished. Take care of yourself." He leaned over the bed and pressed a kiss to her cheek.

"Thanks, Quinn."

He gently squeezed her hand and then went back out to find Seth talking to the tall, dark-haired man he recognized as Michael Hendricks. "She's all yours," he said.

Seth and Michael took over Delores's care while he went to find Danny in the staff lounge where he'd left him. When he came closer, a familiar voice made him slow down and pause just outside the door.

"How do I say, How are you? Like this?" Leila's voice asked.

Danny nodded eagerly, using his small fingers to help Leila's hand form the correct sign of sweeping two fingers up and out from the chest.

"Okay, let me try that again." She pursed her lips in concentration and then made the how-are-you sign, followed by the letters of the alphabet spelling Danny.

How are you, Dr. Leila? Danny asked in response.

His son was teaching Leila sign language. Quinn stared in stunned surprise, warning bells going off in his mind.

She looked so natural with his son, the sight of them brought a lump to the back of his throat. But no matter how good they looked together, he didn't want to go there. He and Danny were doing just fine on their own.

Danny didn't need a mother, he had Delores.

And God knew, the last thing he wanted or needed was a wife.

CHAPTER NINE

QUINN had to clear his tight throat before he could speak. "Hey, Danny. Auntie D. needs to have a procedure that's going to take a few hours so we'll need to stick around the hospital for a while."

Okay. Danny seemed to take the news in his stride.

"Is everything all right?" Leila asked with concern.

"Yes. She was dehydrated from flu and now her cardiac enzymes and troponin are slightly elevated. Michael Hendricks wants to do a cardiac cath just to be sure."

"I see." Leila frowned a bit, and glanced at Danny as if realizing Quinn was glossing over things for his son's sake. "Good thing that test doesn't take long. She'll be finished soon enough, I'd think."

The way she played along only irritated him more, as he hadn't asked for her help. Finding Leila and Danny bonding over sign language bothered him. He didn't want his son to get the wrong idea about Leila. With a strained smile he held out his hand to Danny. "Come on, let's head down to the cafeteria for a while."

Danny scrambled over to his father, but glanced back at Leila. *Can Dr. Leila come, too?*

Quinn was glad his question had been asked in sign language, so Leila wouldn't know what he'd said. "No. Show Dr. Leila how to say goodbye, Danny."

Danny did the universal sign of waving goodbye and Leila laughed, following suit. "Even I can understand that one," she said in a dry tone. "Goodbye, Danny. Hope to see you again some time soon."

Not if he could help it, Quinn thought as he drew Danny away, allowing Leila to go back to work. She had said she wasn't on call, but he knew she had probably stopped in to see her patients.

As he walked with Danny through the arena, he realized there were more important problems than finding Leila with Danny. He was scheduled to work second shift, so he'd need someone to watch Danny from three o'clock until well past eleven. Chances were, even if Delores's cardiac cath was negative, she'd need to stay here overnight for observation. And if she were by some miracle discharged home, she wouldn't be in any condition to watch his son.

Mulling over his dilemma, he decided against going to the cafeteria just yet. Instead, he took Danny to his office. Leaving Danny there to play games on his computer, he went back to find Seth. Asking for help wasn't easy, but he swallowed his pride anyway. "Seth, I, uh, need a favor."

"Hey, I'm glad you're here," Seth said. "Kylie just called to ask if you would mind if Danny stayed overnight with Ben tonight."

An unexpected wave of gratitude hit hard. He didn't for one minute believe Kylie had come up with that idea on her own. Especially considering she and Seth were getting married in two days. Seth, understanding fatherhood more than most, had already anticipated the problem and had arranged for a viable solution before he had the chance to ask.

In that moment Quinn was more thankful than ever that he'd chosen Cedar Bluff to move to. The small town was warm, welcoming and friendly. It wasn't as if he'd had the time to become close to any of the staff here, but Seth and Kylie had come through for him anyway.

The people here were open and honest, seemingly without hidden agendas. Maybe keeping his distance wasn't really necessary after all.

"If you're worried about the sign language issue, I know Ben's been practicing a bit," Seth continued, misunderstanding his silence. "And I can tell you, from watching the boys interact, they seem to communicate pretty well without words. Danny writes simple notes and has always made his needs known. I'm confident we'll be able to communicate just fine."

"Thanks, Seth. I could use some help with Danny tonight, as I am scheduled to work and Delores obviously won't be home." He hesitated and added, "Danny hasn't had the opportunity to participate in any sleepovers, but I think he should be all right." At least, Quinn hoped so. Truthfully, he was a little nervous about having Danny spend the night with people who didn't know sign language, but on the other hand he also trusted Seth and Kylie. Certainly, if they had some sort of problem, they'd call him.

"You know, we live fairly close to the hospital. If anything happens, we'll get in touch with you."

Quinn smiled, knowing Seth had read his thoughts. Again. "I know. Thanks for helping me out."

"Hey, I'm the one who should thank you. With Danny staying over, Ben will be out of our hair for a while." Seth grinned. "Not that I don't love him, but I'd be lying if I said I wouldn't mind a bit of alone time with my future wife, too."

His future wife. Sometimes he forgot that Seth and Kylie weren't officially married yet. They seemed like such a close family unit already. "I can't believe you're getting married in two days," Quinn mused.

"Neither can I." Seth let out an exaggerated sigh. "I'll be glad when the formality of it all is over. I would have been fine with a quick jaunt to Vegas, but Kylie wanted the real deal. And there was no way I was going to disappoint her. I'm lucky enough that she agreed to marry me at all. I hope you'll come to the wedding, too—everyone who works in the department is invited."

Weddings weren't his thing and, truthfully, if he had his way he'd avoid them all together, but Quinn nodded his agreement. From what he'd seen, Seth and Kylie were one of those rare couples who were really, truly in love. Most people weren't nearly so lucky.

He'd long ago accepted his fate. Marriage wasn't for everyone. Some people were better off alone. But he could appreciate those isolated few who seemed determined to make it work. "Sure. Sounds fun."

Seth burst out laughing. "Yeah, right. You say that as if you'd rather have your right foot amputated. Come on, it will be a fun party, if nothing else."

Obviously he hadn't done a good job of hiding his

true feelings. Chagrined, he smiled. "I'll come, don't worry. And I'll be the first to buy the groom a drink."

"Great. And as for tonight, Kylie will stop by to pick up Danny whenever you say the word."

Quinn glanced at the clock. "Maybe we'll wait an hour or so if that's all right. I'd like Danny to see Delores after the procedure, so that he knows she's fine before he goes."

"Understandable," Seth agreed easily. "I'll be here, just give me a holler."

"I will." Quinn headed back to his office to pick up Danny, certain his son would be thrilled to spend the night at Ben's house.

How odd to realize that for the first time in eighteen months he didn't have a reason to hurry home after work.

Danny and Delores would be gone. All night. If he were going to indulge in a secret affair with Leila, this would be the perfect night for it. Too bad he had to work.

But only until eleven. That still left a good portion of the night free and clear.

The idea wouldn't leave him alone. Did he dare call Leila? After the way she'd bonded so easily with Danny, he knew he shouldn't.

But he wanted to. And now that the idea had occurred to him, he couldn't think of anything else.

He very much wanted to invite Leila over.

There was no reason he couldn't, he rationalized. Especially if he made sure she clearly understood the ground rules before he took her to his bed.

* * *

Leila finished her patient rounds, satisfied that things were going as well as could be expected.

Even Carl seemed to be holding his own. Trevor was well on the road to mending. She was pleased he'd been transferred out of the ICU already.

Would Quinn like to know how Trevor was doing? She was tempted to call him, but held back.

He'd acted strangely earlier when he'd discovered Danny had been teaching her some simple sign language. Almost as if he hadn't been pleased to find her keeping his son company.

Although maybe she was simply overreacting. Quinn was obviously upset about Delores and her potential heart problems. And he must be worried, too, about how her illness might have an impact on his child-care arrangements for Danny.

Quinn loved his son very much. Which made her even more curious about Danny's mother. Was she dead? Quinn's comments at dinner the other evening didn't give her the impression he was a grieving widower. Was it possible Danny's mother had abandoned them?

What sort of mother abandoned her child?

A woman like her mother, that's who.

Although, to be fair, the situation was very different. She'd learned her mother had been young, only nineteen when she'd given birth to Leila. Being so young, it was easy to surmise that Maylyn had been a single, unwed mother who had been unable to provide for a child. She had been three months old when her mother had given her up for adoption.

Danny's mother hadn't just given up a son, she'd

given up a guy like Quinn. Did Danny have memories of his mother?

She'd often wished she had some of her own birth mother. But she didn't.

At home, Leila logged onto her computer, automatically checking the reunion Web site that she'd used to post her query, searching for her mother, Maylyn Aquino.

There was a message for her.

Leila stared at the unopened e-mail message for several long seconds, trying not to get her hopes up too high. After all, the person could be just some prankster, not really her mother at all. Taking a deep breath, she finally double-clicked on the message.

"My name is Maylyn Aquino. I'm fifty-three years old and thirty-four years ago, I ran away from home because I was pregnant. While living in Chicago, I tried to support myself and my baby but I couldn't. I left my baby daughter at a local church. If you think you may be my daughter, and if you can forgive me, please write back. Thank you, Maylyn."

Chicago. Local church. Leila felt a chill snake down her spine. She'd grown up in foster care in Chicago and had been told she'd been left at a local church, with just her mother's name and her own as identifiers.

Excitement stole her breath. Could this be it? Was it possible she'd actually found her mother after years of searching? Or was this someone's idea of a sick joke? And if so, why? Why would anyone bother to pretend to be someone they're not? For money? Seemed a stretch, especially as she hadn't posted anything personal about herself. There was no way for anyone to know she was a surgeon, mistakenly thinking she had loads of extra money sitting around.

She desperately wanted to believe. After all this time, to think she might actually learn about her flesh-and-blood family. She could hardly believe it.

With shaking hands, she responded to Maylyn's e-mail. "I grew up in foster care in Chicago and had been left in a church. After going through a few foster homes, I ended up with an older couple who kept me until I graduated from high school. I believe I may be your daughter and would like to know more about my family. Do you have any proof, such as a copy of my birth certificate? If so, I would like to meet you. Thanks, Leila."

She held the blinking arrow hovering over the send key, telling herself she'd be wise to wait, taking the time to make sure this wasn't some sort of prank. But the anticipation was too much to bear and quickly, before she could change her mind, she pressed the send key.

Afterward, she stared at the blank computer screen, wishing she'd asked more questions. Where was her mother living now? What sort of work did she do? Was she married? Did she have more children, providing Leila with some half brothers or sisters?

And most of all, did her mother know who her father was?

She gave herself a mental shake. Too many questions considering she didn't even know for sure Maylyn was her birth mother.

Leila had routine household chores to do, laundry and cleaning, but she couldn't concentrate. She had to force herself not to keep checking the reunion Web site over and over again, looking for a response.

After the fifth time of logging on and finding nothing, Leila realized she'd drive herself crazy if she stayed cooped up in her house with nothing else to do but to stare at her computer. This was why her foster parents hadn't wanted her to search for her birth mother. They hadn't wanted her to obsess like this. But now that they were gone, and George was gone, there was no one to stop her from being foolish.

Thinking of the people she'd loved and lost made her realize she needed to take control of herself. To find something that would keep her mind off the possibility of meeting her birth mother.

She left the house, making her way to the local health club sponsored by Cedar Bluff Hospital. Running on the treadmill helped clear her head, at least for a while. The moment she walked into the house, though, her phone rang. Barely containing a flash of excitement, even though she knew it was impossible for the caller to be her mother, she grabbed the handset. "Hello?"

"Leila?" a deep, familiar male voice asked. "It's Quinn."

"Hello, Quinn. Is everything okay?" She thought it was odd that he'd called her when he was supposed to be working. "How's Danny's caregiver doing?"

"She's fine. Her cardiac cath did show a constricted right main artery, so Michael placed a stent. She's resting comfortably at the moment."

"Good thing they did the cardiac catheterization, so she could get the treatment she needed," Leila said. "Especially as her labs weren't very impressive."

"Absolutely."

"By the way, I thought you'd like to know Trevor was moved out of the ICU today," Leila said. "He's doing great. I'm sure he's going to recover from his injuries just fine."

"I'm glad," Quinn responded. "Thanks for telling me."

"No problem. Carl is holding his own, too, but he's going to be in the ICU for a long while yet."

Quinn didn't say anything, although she was sure he was thinking the guy deserved it. Not that Quinn would wish the man harm, but she knew he'd been far more worried about Carl's young son than the father himself.

"Leila, do you have any plans for later tonight?"

She was glad he was on the other end of the phone and unable to see the shocked expression on her face. It was eight o'clock. "I thought you were working?"

"I am working second shift, I'm on break at the moment. I should be off around eleven or eleven-thirty. I know that's late, but I was hoping you wouldn't mind. Danny's spending the night with Seth and Kylie. We could meet at your place or mine."

Delores was in the hospital recovering from a cardiac cath and Danny was spending the night with a friend. It didn't take much to put two and two together to figure out exactly what Quinn intended.

She supposed she should be glad he hadn't pretended to ask her over for dinner or for a late movie. He was being honest about what he wanted. He planned for her to spend the night. And somehow she didn't think sleeping was on the agenda.

If she agreed to this, she knew she was basically agreeing to have sex with Quinn.

"Leila? Are you still there?"

The note of uncertainty in his tone made her feel a little better. At least he wasn't acting as if making love with her was a foregone conclusion.

"Yes, I'm still here." Wildly she wondered what to do. It was difficult to say no to something she wanted as much as he did. "I guess we could meet later, after your shift."

There was a short pause. "I would really like that, but are you sure? You sound apprehensive."

"Not apprehensive," she assured him. "Just nervous, I guess. It's been a long time for me."

"For me, too." His voice was low, husky. "You have no idea how much I've looked forward to spending time alone with you."

His words sent a tiny thrill of anticipation shimmering through her body. Good grief, she never would have guessed she could react so strongly to him even over the phone. The man's charisma was lethal.

"Do you want me to meet you at the hospital?" she asked.

"How about if I come over to your house instead?"

She licked suddenly dry lips. Instinctively, she thought it would be better to meet him on neutral ground, rather than inviting him into her home, but logically she understood that he might get off later than he'd planned and she'd be sitting around waiting for nothing.

"All right," she said in agreement. "You can meet me here."

"I promise I'll be there as soon as I can." His reverent tone made it impossible to doubt his sincerity.

"I'll see you later, then." She hung up the phone, realizing that the idea of making love with Quinn had managed to trump the excitement of discovering her birth mother.

She wasn't sure which possibility bothered her more.

CHAPTER TEN

QUINN'S shift crept by at an incredibly slow pace. At times it felt as if no time had passed since the last time he'd looked at the clock.

There weren't a lot of patients to see either, which also made the time drag. Twice, he ran up to the cardiac unit to check on Delores, pleased to see she was doing very well. The cardiologist planned on discharging her the following morning, barring any complications from the procedure.

"Where's Danny?" she asked.

"Having a sleepover with Ben, Seth and Kylie." He'd told her about Danny's plans earlier, but she'd been under the influence of pain medication at the time, so he didn't blame her for not remembering.

"Good. That's good."

He was a little surprised she didn't make any cracks about his social life, and the fact that he had the rest of the night free of parental responsibilities. She also didn't seem to notice anything different about him, despite him feeling as if he had a neon sign plastered to his forehead that flashed, *I'm having sex with Leila tonight.*

At least, he hoped he was having sex with Leila tonight. If he didn't mess things up. And if she didn't have a change of heart while waiting for him.

He should be glad Delores hadn't noticed, because he had promised Leila he'd be discreet. It would be just his luck for Delores to blurt out the truth while picking up Danny at school.

Reassured that Delores was in good hands, he headed back down to the ED. Another patient had come in, but only a young mother with a minor laceration, the result of two kids playing football in the house and a broken mirror. A complex multiple trauma would have made the time pass, but he couldn't be callous enough to hope some poor soul would get hurt.

As the end of his shift finally drew near, he found himself watching the clock even more closely and hoping this time that a major trauma *didn't* roll through the doors at the last minute, since that would definitely make him late for his date with Leila.

He didn't want to give her any opportunity to change her mind about seeing him. About spending the night with him.

Thankfully, the trauma pager remained quiet and Jadon arrived for his night shift promptly on time. Quinn bolted from the hospital, rushing over to Leila's house, but he was standing on her front porch when he belatedly noticed there weren't many lights on inside.

Had she fallen asleep?

Would she hear his knock? And if so, would she let him in or simply tell him to get lost?

He rapped sharply on the door and held his breath,

praying she'd answer. He was just about to knock again, louder this time, when the door opened.

"Hi, Quinn," she said with a shy smile.

Light-headed with relief, he stepped inside the warmth of her home. She was beautiful, her long straight dark hair loose around her shoulders and her curvy figure showcased perfectly in a stretchy knit cream-colored sweater and black leggings. He had to talk himself out of picking her up and tossing her over his shoulder to search for the closest bedroom.

"Thanks for waiting up for me." Now that he was here, he felt awkward. He hadn't been kidding when he'd told her earlier that he hadn't done this in a long time.

Years. Too many years to count.

She closed the door behind him. "I'll take your coat. Would you like something to drink? I have beer and wine."

He noticed a half-full glass of wine next to a laptop computer on the end table beside the sofa, surmising it was hers. "Wine, if that's what you're drinking."

"All right. Have a seat, I'll be right back." She disappeared into the kitchen.

He wandered over to look at the computer, seeing a search engine up on the screen. His stomach tightened with apprehension. Had she searched for information about Danny's mother?

No. If Leila had known, she'd have asked him about it. He'd learned from the incident with Trevor's mother that Leila didn't hesitate to confront him if she felt the need.

And now that he was here, how did he broach the subject of their affair? He'd made his intention clear during dinner a couple of nights ago, but in his opinion, a guy couldn't be too careful. Best for Leila to go into this affair with her eyes wide open and her expectations reasonable.

"Here you go," she said, returning to the living room with another glass of wine. "I hope you like Merlot."

"I do." He took the wine from her fingers, feeling a bit like a clumsy oaf next to her daintiness. "Have you been working?" he asked, gesturing to the computer.

"Just researching." She shrugged and closed the computer, effectively shutting it off. "I've been staring at the screen for so long, my eyes are blurry."

"I don't know much about computers," he confessed, taking a seat on her comfortable sofa. "It's scary to think Danny will pass me in another year or two."

She laughed as she sank down next to him, sending a stab of desire shooting straight to his groin. "You're like my husband. He didn't have much use for computers either."

Her husband. Not his favorite topic, but he could maybe gently remind her about his no-future rules in a roundabout way. "How long were you married?"

"Two years." Her smile was melancholy and he wondered if she missed her husband at times like this, especially around the holidays. "I'm thankful for the time I had with him, though."

"You didn't have children?" He knew he was probing into dangerous territory, but he couldn't help himself. He was more curious about her than he had a right to be.

"No. George wanted them, but I didn't think it was fair."

He frowned. Most women he knew wanted babies. Celeste, especially, had wanted a large family. But that had been before one child had proven to be too much. Oh, at first she'd been thrilled to have Danny, but then him working too many hours, leaving her alone with a small baby, had taken its toll. By the time Danny was two, she'd sunk into deep depression. By the time he'd been four and a half, she'd taken her own life. "Because of your career?"

She shook her head. "Because I don't know anything about my past, including my family health history. Are my genes prone to cancer? Heart disease? Psychiatric disorders? Neurological diseases? What if I have some obscure genetic illness that I haven't discovered yet?" She took a sip of her wine, her gaze pensive. "Now that George is gone, it's probably for the best that we didn't have children."

He didn't necessarily agree. His life wouldn't be worth living if not for Danny. He wouldn't ever regret marrying Celeste because she'd given him the gift of their son. He and Danny were a team. But for now he thought it was best to play along. "You're probably right. Being a single parent is challenging."

"Yes, although you and Danny appear to have a great relationship," she mused.

"We do. And that's the main reason I'm not looking for anything more." He glanced at her, hoping he hadn't sounded too blunt. "Leila, I want you, very much. But I need to tell you, I can't offer you a future."

He winced when her eyes flashed with hurt. But then the moment of pain was gone and her chin lifted defiantly. "I don't remember asking for a future."

He should have been relieved, but instead he was vexed at her tone. Why wouldn't she want a future with him? Because he didn't measure up to her precious George? What had been so wonderful about her first husband? And so what if he didn't measure up to the guy? Ridiculous to be jealous of a dead man.

"You didn't. I'm sorry, please give me a chance to start over." He reached across and took her glass of wine away, setting it on the end table next to his. Then he took her hand, cradling it in his as he edged closer. "Leila, I've been looking forward to seeing you all evening."

"Oh, really?" Her dry tone said she didn't believe him, but her pupils dilated in response when he lifted her hand and brushed his mouth across her knuckles.

"Yes. You have no idea how long I've waited for this." He turned her hand so he could press another lingering kiss on the delicate skin covering the pulse of her wrist. "It's a good thing I didn't have any complicated patients, as I couldn't concentrate worth a damn. All I could think of was you. Us."

"You don't have to seduce me," she protested, in a husky tone. "I invited you here, remember?"

If any woman needed seduction, it was Leila. She was a complex mix of experience, brilliance, tenderheartedness and innocence. He didn't understand exactly what was going on in that brain of hers, but he sensed she was unsure of herself, or at least unsure of the situation.

Which meant he needed to take his time, until she was comfortable with him.

He didn't mind. After all, they had all night.

* * *

Leila wondered if it was too late to back out of their arrangement. She'd almost canceled a dozen times while waiting for Quinn to get off work. And from the moment he'd arrived, she'd suspected they were making a mistake.

Him reinforcing this was nothing more than an affair didn't help her feel any better.

Yet she couldn't make herself send him away. And when he tugged the sleeve of her sweater up and pressed his hot mouth to the inside of her elbow, she nearly gasped.

Since when had the inside of her elbow been an erogenous zone? And how many other erogenous zones did she possess that she was unaware of?

"Remember the night I massaged your feet?" he asked in a low murmur.

The way his mouth moved against her skin, causing every nerve ending to sizzle, made it difficult to think. "Yes."

"I'd like to do that again, only this time I'd work my way upward until you were completely naked and I've had the opportunity to massage every glorious inch of your body."

The thought of him doing exactly that was intoxicating. Her heart thundered in her ears, making her dizzy. His hands and his mouth teased and tortured her simultaneously.

"That sounds very…one-sided," she finally managed. Lifting her hand, she threaded her fingers through his dark hair, urging him to continue his heady exploration. "I think this is supposed to be a mutually rewarding experience."

He let out a low, husky laugh. "Trust me, I'll enjoy every minute of pleasuring you."

When he said things like that, she almost believed him. His mouth found the tender skin along her jaw, his hand pushing up the hem of her sweater until he could caress the bare skin of her abdomen. She dropped her head back to give him greater access to her neck and wondered what it would be like if he kissed her there on her stomach, too.

No man had ever treated her like this, as if every inch of her body intrigued him. Excited him. Thrilled him. She ran her hand up his arm, squeezing his shoulder as she urged him closer. They were still on her sofa, although she was lounging back, trying to pull Quinn on top of her. He didn't seem to be in a rush to get her into bed, but took his time as he nuzzled, nipped and licked her neck, her throat, even the hidden spot behind her ear, before claiming her mouth with his.

Her entire body shimmered with tension, and she wished she'd greeted him at the door wearing nothing but her birthday suit because their clothes were definitely in the way.

"Quinn, please," she begged, wishing she could explore his body the way he was touching her. The hardness of his muscles cushioning her softness felt wonderful but she wanted more. She tugged at his shirt, dragging it up his back. "I want you."

"God, Leila," he said with a groan when she finally succeeded in yanking his shirt over his head and tossing the inside-out garment to the floor before smoothing her hands over the rock-hard muscles of his chest. "Not as much as I want you."

Wanna bet? she thought with a secret smile. Her smile faded when he stripped her sweater off and kissed her stomach, sending a jolt of electricity straight to the already moist juncture of her thighs.

Her humorous thoughts were quickly replaced with serious, urgent desire. As Quinn deftly opened her front-clasp bra, freeing her breasts, she dimly realized she was close to having an orgasm and he hadn't even taken all her clothes off yet.

"My bedroom," she gasped. "First door on the right."

He lifted his head, gazing intently down at her. "We'll get to the bedroom soon enough, don't worry."

His *soon* wasn't soon enough for her. He began peeling off her leggings, and she helped the best she could, given her rather awkward position on the sofa. "Now, Quinn. There isn't enough room on this sofa."

"There's plenty of room." His piercing gaze stroked her nearly naked body and she'd never before had a man look at her with such appreciation and longing. "At least for what I have in mind. I have to say, there's nothing as delicious as a good antipasto."

An appetizer? Like the sampling before the main meal? She was almost afraid to ask. But then he kissed her bare breasts, moved lower to her quivering abdomen and her breath lodged in her throat when he moved lower still, drawing her underwear out of the way.

She wanted to protest. Her sex life with George hadn't included this level of intimacy, but Quinn's mouth felt so good, she couldn't find the words to ask him to stop.

And then she couldn't speak at all, even if she wanted to. Couldn't stop herself from responding to his most intimate touch by raising her hips higher, silently urging him on, lost in the sensation until the curling tension exploded with an unprecedented rush. "Quinn!"

"Shh," he soothed between kisses as he gently worked his way back up her body. "It's all right, *quierda*. We have all night."

All night? The very thought made her feel weak. Somehow she knew he was completely serious, not one bit overstating his ability to make love all night long.

And suddenly a trickle of concern made its way into her pleasure-soaked brain.

She already felt closer to Quinn than she should. For him, this was just a sexual diversion.

For her, it had the potential to become more.

"Come, *quierda*," he said, drawing her upright from where she'd been sprawled on the sofa. "First door on the right?"

"Yes." She barely recognized her hoarse croak.

He must have noticed her moment of indecision because he swept her into his arms, stepping over their discarded clothing as he carried her to the bedroom, like a pirate striding off with his booty.

He set her down and she was grateful for the darkness, as only the little bit of light from the living room illuminated the room. Her pirate didn't disregard her feelings, though. Instead, he smoothed her hair away from her damp face. "Are you okay?" he murmured.

His concern made her want to smile.

"Fine." He held her close enough that she could feel the hard evidence of his arousal. And, impossibly, she felt the desperate need to have him, all over again. "Perfect. Couldn't be better."

"Good." He put a little distance between them to shuck off the rest of his clothing until he was as naked as she. Quinn without clothes was breathtaking and now she wished for the light so she could see him better.

Reaching out, she stroked her hands over his chest, relishing the way he sucked in a harsh breath when she moved her hands lower, over his abdomen. "I think it's my turn."

"Our turn," he corrected, putting his hands on hers as if to stop her. He tried to nudge her toward the bed.

"My turn," she insisted, moving her hands lower still, until she could wrap her hand around him.

"Leila," he groaned when she gently squeezed and stroked. "You're killing me."

Bringing him pleasure only made her want him more. And suddenly she understood what he'd meant when he'd told her that he'd enjoy every minute of her full body massage. Making love like this was good for both of them.

"Come to bed with me, Quinn," she whispered.

He crushed her close, kissing her deeply as they tumbled to the mattress. He braced himself above her, their limbs entwined, but she tried to pull him closer, anxious to feel the weight of him against her.

"Wait," he muttered, when she wrapped her legs around his waist. "Condom."

She almost whimpered when he pulled away, reaching for his pants on the floor to dig the necessary foil packet out of his pocket. Good thing he'd remembered because protection hadn't been at the forefront in her mind. Still, she took the condom from him, and prolonged the pleasure by slowly rolling the latex protection over him.

At that moment the thin thread of his control snapped. He groaned low in his throat as he rocked her backward against the bed, urgently spreading her legs and thrusting deep.

Yes! This was what she'd wanted. He pulled out and thrust again, harder, and she welcomed him, wrapping her legs around him and clinging to his shoulders as he set the pace.

And this time, when the explosion came, they were both in it together.

Afterward, she was surprised when he rolled to the side, holding her close, as if loath to let her go.

Afraid to say anything to ruin the afterglow of pleasure, she curled up beside him, loving the reassuring sound of his heartbeat beneath her ear.

A tiny part of her mind wanted to believe Quinn cared about her more than he'd let on.

Because surely if this was nothing more than an affair, he'd already be out the door heading back to his house, not cuddled up next to her like this.

CHAPTER ELEVEN

EARLY the next morning, she awoke and stretched luxuriously, her body tender and sore in several places but unable to muster the energy to care. She felt good. Wickedly good. Quinn had made love to her several times in the wee hours of the morning before they'd both fallen into a deep sleep.

But now their night together was over. She glanced over at Quinn, his hair black against her cream-colored pillows, thinking how long it had been since she'd shared her bed with a man. And being with Quinn had been so different from what she'd been used to.

Since thinking of George, even fleetingly, made her feel guilty, she quickly pushed those thoughts away. George had always wanted her to be happy.

The covers had slipped down, exposing Quinn's bare chest. She'd kissed and stroked that beautiful body of his all night, but now just looking at him thrilled her.

As if he felt her gaze on him, Quinn stirred, rolling toward her and opening his eyes halfway. A satisfied male smile tugged the corner of his lips. "*Quierda,*" he murmured, pulling her close for a kiss and then tucking her beside him.

"Good morning," she said breathlessly, her body tingling with awareness when she'd thought it would be impossible to want him again after their nonstop love-making last night. She pressed her face into the hollow of his shoulder, breathing in his musky, unique scent and wishing they could spend the rest of the day together, just like this.

Well, maybe with the occasional break for meals, as she was starving. She imagined they'd burned more than the average amount of calories last night with the strength of their passion.

Ignoring the gnawing in her stomach, she kissed his neck, her mouth lingering on his skin. Maybe he wouldn't have to go just yet.

"Leila, you'd tempt the celibacy of a monk," he said with a low groan, pulling away so he could look down at her. "As much as I want to stay, I need to leave. Michael Hendricks told me he'd discharge Delores today and I promised to pick up Danny first thing. She'll expect us to be there soon."

She swallowed a lump of disappointment. She'd known he'd planned to leave early, so she nodded and tried to offer a smile. "I know."

Her smile must have been a little pathetic, because he stared down at her, his expression intent and serious. "I don't want to leave you like this."

Her heart swelled with hope at his words, and some of the pain of his leaving eased away. The expression in his eyes made her feel cherished. "It's okay. I understand."

He lowered his mouth for another searing kiss and she wrapped her arms around his neck, pulling him close, pressing her bare breasts against his chest. He plundered her mouth with his, igniting sensual fires that danced all the way down her spine.

His arousal pressed insistently against her hip. Knowing how easily she could stimulate him gave her a secret thrill. She thought he'd give in, make love to her one last time, but instead he broke away, breathing hard.

"I have to go," he said with a low groan, pulling out of her arms and sitting up in the bed. He scrubbed his hands over his face. "I'm sorry."

She couldn't answer, a hard lump of regret lodged in her throat. She watched as he slipped from her bed, picked up his pants and walked fully naked into her bathroom.

The door closed behind him with a soft click and she squeezed her eyes shut, refusing to cry. Ridiculous to feel as if he was deserting her. After all, this was what they'd both agreed to. An affair.

Lust wasn't love. How many times did she have to remind herself of that fact? This burning intensity she felt with Quinn wasn't the sort of emotion that lasted through the years until the end of time. This was nothing like the love she'd shared with George.

Quinn was right to leave now.

She used the time while he was in the bathroom to get out of bed, dressing in comfortable jeans and sweater. She needed to take a shower, but that could wait until after Quinn was gone. She went into the kitchen to start a pot of coffee.

Quinn came out a few minutes later, pulling on his wrinkled shirt, which had been left in a heap on her living-room floor.

She strove to sound casual. "Would you like a cup of coffee before you go?"

"No, thanks," he said, looking at her with sincere regret. "If I stay much longer, I'm afraid I won't leave at all."

She wanted to tell him he was welcome to come back any time, but knew that wouldn't be wise. He was a man with responsibilities. She knew, without being told, he'd never stay over with her like this while his son was at home.

And how many sleepovers could Danny have without raising suspicions?

"All right, I'll get your coat." She brushed past him to head into the living room to pull his coat from the closet.

"Leila, I've been invited to Seth and Kylie's wedding tomorrow evening on New Year's Eve," he said as he took the coat from her and shrugged into it. "Would you like to come with me?"

Her brows rose in surprise. Him inviting her to go out with him again was the last thing she'd expected. And as much as she would have loved to go, being with him might be a bit obvious. "I've been invited to their wedding, too," she admitted. "I'm not on call that night, so I'm sure I'll see you there."

He stared at her again and then nodded. "I'll look forward to it."

Pasting a brave smile on her face, she opened the front door. "Goodbye, Quinn."

"Bye, Leila." He looked as if he wanted to kiss her again, but after a brief hesitation he turned and left.

She closed the door behind him, dropping her forehead against the cool, smooth wood frame and closing her eyes in a wave of despair.

Maybe it would be best to avoid seeing Quinn again as she was beginning to think she didn't have the ability to indulge in an affair.

Not without opening herself up to a world of hurt.

Quinn had to force himself to keep walking away from Leila, down the step to her driveway where he'd left his car, when every nerve in his body wanted nothing more but to turn back, to stay with her.

He scraped the ice off his windshield with more force than necessary, and then drove home to change clothes, shivering in the cold and missing Leila's warmth. His stomach churned and he wondered if it was because he was missing Leila already.

The house was eerily empty. The silence bothered him. He'd gotten used to coming home to Danny and Delores. Even late at night, he always knew they were there. Striding through the living room, he headed to his room and the adjoining bathroom to shower, regretfully washing away the lingering scent of Leila and their lovemaking from his skin. Images of their night together arose in his mind and he groaned, remembering her touch as he soaped his body.

He had to stop torturing himself like this. Obviously one night with Leila wasn't enough. She was still firmly lodged in his system, and he was unable to shake her loose.

He should have been fine. A night full of steamy, immensely satisfying sex should have been enough to dull the edge of need.

So why did he feel as if he'd never have enough?

Shaking his head at his folly, he turned off the shower and dried off before searching for clean clothes to wear. His stomach didn't feel so good and, thinking he was hungry, he ate a bowl of cold cereal before calling Seth to make sure everything was fine with Danny.

Seth answered cheerfully, reassuring Quinn that all was fine. He promised to have Danny ready to go by the time Quinn got there.

After hanging up with Seth, he called the hospital. He had to wait a few minutes to be connected to Delores's room, but then she answered the phone. "Hello?"

"Delores, it's Quinn. How are you feeling?"

"Good. Anxious to get out of here."

"Great." He was glad to hear she sounded like her old self. The flu bug must only last twenty-four hours. "I'll pick up Danny first, and then we'll be out to pick you up."

"Okay, but you haven't forgotten about Danny's therapist appointment this morning, have you?" Delores asked anxiously. "Dr. Adams is expecting him at ten-thirty."

With a guilty start he glanced at the calendar posted on the fridge. He had forgotten. Delores was usually the one who took Danny to his appointments, although he'd met with Nancy himself when they'd first arrived in Cedar Bluff. Danny usually met with her twice a week but, considering this was the week between Christmas and New Year, Nancy had requested to cut back to just one day. Today. "I'll get him to the clinic, don't worry."

"All right, if you're sure."

He was sure they'd be cutting it close if Delores wasn't ready to be discharged by the time he arrived at the hospital. On the way to Seth's he called Michael Hendricks to explain the situation.

"I'll have everything ready to go," Michael promised. "Her discharge paperwork will be complete and I'll have the nurses help her get dressed right now, so there won't be any delay."

"Thanks." Grateful for Michael's understanding, he hung up the phone and stood, feeling worse than before. Since his appetite had vanished, he gave up on the cold cereal, dumping the remains in the sink. His head and his stomach hurt and he figured he wouldn't be himself until he had Danny and Delores back home where they both belonged.

Pulling his coat back on, he headed over to pick up Danny. Danny was obviously excited about his sleepover, his fingers flying through sign language that Quinn had trouble keeping up with as he navigated the road. At times like this he would have given anything to hear the chatter of Danny's voice.

"You beat Ben how many times?" he asked, trying to follow Danny's convoluted sentences. "Seven?"

Danny gave an exasperated sigh and tried again.

"Oh, sorry. Five times. That's amazing. I'm glad you had fun."

How is Auntie D. doing?

"Great. We're picking her up from the hospital now, and then we'll take her home. You have a doctor's appointment with Dr. Adams at ten-thirty."

Danny scrunched up his face.

"What's wrong?" he asked, a little concerned. "I thought you liked going to see her."

Danny shrugged and then launched into another sign-language discussion about the games he and Ben had played.

Quinn parked in the doctors' parking lot and they walked inside. His legs felt heavy, like they were filled with lead, probably a result of his late night and very little sleep. His head still ached and his stomach didn't feel great either. The cold cereal he'd eaten earlier sloshed uncomfortably in his gut.

His fault, though, for keeping Leila up half the night making love to her, so he wasn't going to complain. Good thing he had the day off, though. The way he felt right now, he wouldn't be able to work.

He and Danny rode the elevator to the fourth floor, finding Delores in her room, dressed and ready to go as promised.

In no time at all, Quinn had Delores and Danny bundled up in his car and was heading home. Inside, he made sure Delores was settled comfortably in her room before hustling Danny back out for his doctor's appointment.

"Wait, what about lunch?" Delores asked as he started to leave.

"I'll take Danny out for lunch, you just rest."

"All right," she said with a huff, settling back in her bed. "But I'm not an invalid, you know."

"Of course you aren't." He barely refrained from rolling his eyes in disgust. What part of having the flu and a subsequent mild heart attack didn't she understand? Sure, she wasn't an invalid, but she wasn't Superwoman either.

He flipped through several magazines as he sat in the small room, waiting for Danny to finish with Nancy Adams. When she saw him there with Danny, she'd agreed to talk to him after the appointment to bring him up to speed on Danny's progress.

Quinn's head throbbed painfully, causing the words to go blurry at times. And the sick feeling in his stomach persisted. Was he hungry? Food didn't necessarily appeal, but then again he hadn't eaten much that morning or the night before.

Ignoring his discomfort, he tried to concentrate on the magazine article he was reading. It was an article about a young man who'd been adopted and had eventually been reunited with his birth parents.

The article reminded him of Leila. After the night of intimacy they'd spent together, he still didn't know very much about her. Was she trying to find her birth parents, too? He tore the article out of the magazine and folded it up into his pocket so he could give it to her when he saw her again.

"Dr. Torres?"

He glanced up to see Nancy Adams standing there next to Danny. He hastily rose to his feet, hiding a flash of dizziness. "Yes?"

"We're finished. Danny, have a seat here for a few minutes while I talk to your dad, all right?"

Danny nodded and crutch-walked over to the table full of children's books. He picked one out and settled down to read.

Feeling somewhat apprehensive, Quinn followed

Nancy Adams into her office. "So, how is Danny doing?"

She pursed her lips a bit as she sat down across from him. "Actually, I wanted to ask how you were doing first."

"Me?" He was taken aback by her question. "I'm fine. Why would you think there's something wrong? Did Danny say something?"

"No, Danny didn't say anything. But you lost your wife, Dr. Torres, at the same time Danny lost his mother. Doesn't that give me the right to ask how you're doing?"

He shifted uncomfortably in his seat. "Yes, I suppose so, but I really am fine. That last year with Celeste was very difficult. I know her illness was partially my fault, but I've accepted it and have moved on. It's Danny who concerns me. It's been eighteen months and he still hasn't said a word."

Nancy Adams was an attractive woman in her late fifties, but the way she looked at him now, so intently, he wondered if she could see through him, all the way to the depths of his soul. Did she suspect he'd spent the night in Leila's arms? Did moving on from the nightmare with Celeste make him a bad person?

"Danny is doing very well," she said finally, dropping the subject of him for the moment. "Today, in particular, he seemed more animated than usual."

Quinn nodded. "He spent the night with a friend last night, and I must admit I've never seen him so excited either."

"Danny really has been making progress with his friends, and I think for the first time in a long time he's finding his lack of speech a barrier. A few times I've caught him looking very frustrated, as if he wanted to blurt something out."

A shiver of excitement raced through him. "That's good news."

"Yes. As I've said before, Danny will speak again when he's ready. You're raising a very well-adjusted child. Whatever you're doing," she added with a gentle smile, "keep it up."

Like making love with Leila? No, she meant with Danny. Getting Danny involved more with his class-mates. Like the sledding trip and this most recent sleep-over. Being home more with his son. Keeping their small family intact. "I will."

"Good. We'll start back up with his twice-a-week schedule on Tuesdays and Thursdays next week."

"All right." Quinn rose to his feet and held out a hand. "Thanks, Dr. Adams, for everything."

She shook her head as she took his hand in a firm grip. "Don't thank me yet, not until Danny's started talking."

After his discussion with Nancy Adams, Quinn was convinced Danny would start talking again very soon.

He could be patient. And no matter what, he didn't want to give Danny any setbacks. He didn't dare intro-duce anything new into their lives at this point.

"Ready for lunch?" he asked, when he returned to the waiting room to pick up Danny. "We can go to which-ever fast-food restaurant you want."

Mr. Burger? Danny asked.

"Sure. Why not?" Quinn knew the local burger joint was his son's favorite mostly because of the giant indoor play area.

Because the kids were all off school this week, the place was packed. He found a seat near the play area, so he could keep an eye on Danny, who scoffed his food in record time so he'd have time to hang out in the play area.

Quinn stared at his burger, feeling nauseous again. He put a hand to his head, surprised to find he was sweating. What in the heck was wrong with him? Losing sleep had never made him feel this lousy.

Whatever it was, he needed to get home, so he wouldn't be sick in front of Danny. He found the restroom and threw up the bit of food he'd managed to get down. After a few minutes he went back out to the play area to look for his son. The room swam dizzily, forcing him to grab on to the back of the chair to keep his balance. Light-headed, he blinked, locking his knees to stay upright.

He was damned if he'd fall on his face here amidst the horde of parents, a few of whom were glancing at him with curiosity, but he needed to get home. Soon.

"Danny?" he called, forcing his voice to carry over the noise. "Come on, we need to get going."

Danny's face fell, but he eventually headed over to stand by his father.

Quinn was sweating profusely now, his clothes sticking uncomfortably to his skin. He didn't understand what was wrong. He never got sick. Ever. He led Danny outside to his car, praying he'd find the strength to drive home.

He gripped the steering wheel in his sweaty hands and for a moment considered calling Leila to come and get them. No, that wasn't fair. Wasn't he the one who'd insisted they had no future? And now he wanted her help? He couldn't have it both ways.

Turning on the car engine, he squinted through the windshield and decided the hospital was closer. His stomach lurched again. He was sick. He might have caught Delores's flu bug. Maybe he just needed a liter or two of IV fluids to feel better.

He had to blink several times to keep the road in focus as he drove the short couple of blocks to the hospital. He was very careful, not wanting to cause an accident yet feeling like his brain was becoming dissociated from his body.

"Danny, we need to stop here at the hospital for a minute," he said, pulling up to the entrance of the ED. His voice sounded far away, as if he were at the other end of a long tunnel. "I need some medicine. I think I have the flu."

He opened his car door and pushed himself upright. His knees buckled and his head spun. He grabbed the car door to hold himself upright so he wouldn't fall face-first into the slush.

He felt Danny scramble out of the car, hobbling next to him with his crutches. He wanted to reassure his son he was all right, but he couldn't see Danny. Everything was blurry.

He wasn't sick. He didn't ever get sick. What in the hell was going on? He told himself to walk, to get inside the hospital, out of the cold, but his legs wouldn't obey. Instead, he found himself sliding downward as his muscles gave away like flimsy straw.

He dropped his chin to his chest, fighting off a wave of darkness. He couldn't pass out. He couldn't.

Dammit, don't do this, he told himself. Get up. Don't scare Danny.

Don't scare Danny!

With a herculean effort, he staggered to his feet. He took a few steps, but then leaned heavily against the hood of his car. The ED was only a few feet away, but his gaze kept fading out and all too soon he found himself sliding down to the ground once again.

"Daddy?" He thought he was imagining his son's voice. But then it came again, louder, a shrill cry, just as darkness threatened.

"Daddy! Help! Somebody help my daddy!"

CHAPTER TWELVE

"DADDY!" The sound of a child's cry distracted Leila from her patient. Then she heard the voice again, louder. "Somebody help my daddy!"

The stab wound on her patient wasn't too serious or life-threatening, so she quickly slapped a sterile dressing over the area to keep it clean before stripping off her gloves and striding to the ED entranceway with Melanie, one of the ED nurses, following close behind.

"Danny?" She stared in surprise, hardly able to believe the boy calling for help was actually Danny Torres. But then she noticed the car sitting with its doors open and the crumpled figure of Quinn lying next to it.

"Melanie, get a stretcher. Quick!" Leila hurried to Quinn, kneeling beside him and feeling for a pulse. Quinn's skin was cool and clammy, but the reassuring beat of his heart, even if it was beating far too fast, gave her hope. She strove to hide the extent of her panicky fear. "Quinn? Can you hear me?"

"Danny," he whispered. His eyes were still closed so she couldn't tell if he'd heard her or if he was confused and delirious.

"Danny is here." She glanced up and met Danny's wide, frightened gaze. She gestured for him to come closer. "Danny's here and he's fine."

Actually, Danny didn't look fine. He looked pale and sick, like his father. He was standing without his crutches and she tugged him close to her side, giving him a reassuring hug. As much as she wanted to ask him to speak, like he had when he'd called out for help, she didn't want to push the issue either.

"Put your hand on his arm, Danny," she said in a low voice. "Let him know you're here."

Danny awkwardly lowered himself to the ground, doing what she asked, staying near his father until Melanie arrived with the stretcher and several more of the ED staff, including Jadon Reichert, who was the ED attending physician in charge. As everyone crowded around Quinn, she picked Danny up, moving him out of the way so they could lift Quinn onto the stretcher.

Quinn didn't open his eyes, even when they'd wheeled him inside. Leila fetched his crutches from the car and kept Danny with her as they followed Quinn to the nearest trauma bay. There was no sign of her stab-wound patient. She thought he must have been moved to the arena.

"Get me a set of vitals and start a peripheral IV," Jadon snapped, his tension evident as he glanced around the room. "We also need a baseline set of labs. Does anyone know what happened before he fell?"

A history of signs and symptoms would be helpful, but with Danny not talking, she wasn't sure they'd get anything helpful. But she'd seen Quinn early that morning. Obviously, this wasn't the time to worry about gossip or her reputation. Leila swallowed hard and forced herself to speak up. "I spent the night with Quinn last night. He seemed fine when he left early this morning."

Jadon's gaze didn't register shock or amusement, and she was thankful her personal life wasn't his prime concern at the moment. Instead, he looked upset. "If he was fine this morning, what in the heck happened between then and now?"

Danny's hand slid into hers, his fingers tightening around hers. She glanced down at him in surprise. "Danny? Do you know what happened? Did your dad say anything before he fell?"

There was a long pause as Danny stared up at her imploringly, as if he wanted to talk but couldn't. Helplessly, Leila wondered if there was a sign language interpreter they could get hold of. They needed to know what, if anything, Danny knew. Without having information about Quinn's signs and symptoms, they didn't have a clue how to diagnose or treat him.

"We need a sign language interpreter," she said to Melanie. "Can you get hold of one stat?"

Melanie nodded, heading for the nearest phone.

"He said he needed medicine." Danny's voice was so quiet Leila had to bend closer to hear him.

"He said he needed medicine?" she asked with a puzzled frown, not sure if she'd heard the boy correctly.

He nodded.

She held his gaze with hers, smiling at him reassuringly. "That's great, Danny. That helps us out. Do you know what medicine your dad takes?"

Danny looked distressed as he shook his head. "He said he thought he had flu."

"Flu?" Then it hit her. Of course, Dolores had been sick the day before. Only in her case, being so dehydrated had caused a mild heart attack.

"He might have flu," she said to Jadon. "Remember how Danny's Aunt Delores came in yesterday with the same sort of symptoms? And we've been hearing for weeks that the flu strain hitting the public this year is one of the worst ever."

"Blood pressure is low, 95 over 44, and his pulse is tachy at 118," Susan, the other trauma nurse, announced.

"Open up those IV fluids," Jadon said. "And get him connected to the heart monitor. Let's make sure he's not throwing any funky heartbeats. I want to know the results of his electrolytes now."

"I'll get them," Melanie said, picking up the receiver from where she'd set it down after Danny had started talking. Leila could hear her telling the lab tech she wanted the electrolyte results now, not in five minutes. *Now.*

"Thanks for telling us what your dad said, Danny," Leila said, crouching down so she was at eye level with Quinn's son. She flashed him a broad smile. "With your help we know exactly what to do to make your dad feel better."

"Will he wake up?" Danny asked, his tone barely above a whisper.

Her heart clenched for this small boy, who'd undoubtedly gone through hell thinking the worst when his father had collapsed on the ground. Even if the shock had helped him find his voice, remnants of fear still haunted his dark eyes.

"Yes, Danny. I think your dad is going to be fine." At least, she hoped so. Unless there was some medication that Quinn had been taking that they didn't know about? She gave Danny a gentle, reassuring hug and then stood up.

"See if Quinn has a medical record on file," Leila said to Melanie. "Hopefully we'll find out what medications, if any, he's on." She knew nothing about Quinn's past medical history.

"Okay, but first I have his electrolyte results. His potassium is low at 2.6 and the chloride is low, too. Even his magnesium is low."

"Hang twenty milieqivalents of potassium chloride and add another twenty to his liter of IV fluids." Jadon snapped orders like a drill sergeant, but no one seemed to mind. "Give him a second dose of potassium before the magnesium supplement. Keep an eye on those premature ventricular beats and let me know if he has more than 16 a minute."

"Dr. Ross?" Leila glanced at Melanie. "There are no medical records for Dr. Torres on file."

Damn. Did that mean Quinn didn't have any previous medical problems? Or that he just hadn't used Cedar Bluff Hospital, the clinic or the pharmacy to renew his prescriptions? He'd only been in Cedar Bluff for a month or maybe a little longer. He may not have taken the time to transfer his prescriptions to the hospital pharmacy. "Okay, thanks for checking."

At that moment Quinn stirred. He let out a low groan and opened his eyes, then shut them again, turning away from the bright overhead lights. "Tell me I'm not in the ED," he said in a low, strangled voice.

Her lips twitched with relief. Waking up in the emergency department where you worked was every physician's worst nightmare.

"Okay, I won't tell you," Jadon said, his tense expression easing a bit. "Maybe you'd like to tell us what happened?"

"Where's Danny?" True to form, Quinn's attention quickly shifted to his son.

"Danny's right here," Leila said, stepping forward, bringing Danny with her. She glanced down at Danny with a reassuring smile. "Danny was a huge help. He told us you felt like you had flu and that you needed some medication."

Quinn's eyes snapped open, even if his gaze didn't seem entirely focused as he swiveled his head in her direction. "He did?"

Her smile was broad. "Yes, he did. But you need to clue us in here, Quinn. We're flying a little blind. Exactly what medication do you need?"

"No meds, I meant IV fluids. Whatever you've given me is working. I'm already feeling better." He looked at his son. "Danny? How are you? Are you doing all right?"

She tried to nudge Danny closer to Quinn's stretcher, but he leaned on his crutches, glued to her side. The boy nodded in response to his father's question and she could tell Quinn was disappointed he didn't say anything.

She frowned and tried to warn Quinn with her gaze

not to make a big deal about it. "I'll keep Danny with me for a while, until you're feeling better."

Quinn's eyes widened with alarm. "No!" At her shocked expression he hastened to add, "I mean, I want him to stay here. With me."

"Sure. I understand." She hid her flash of disappointment, not sure why Quinn was being so protective about Danny, especially after the boy had made huge strides by talking, not just once during the height of the emergency when he'd called for help but then again a second time when they'd needed to know what was wrong with Quinn. Glancing down at Danny, who looked far less afraid now that his dad was awake and talking, she said, "Danny, your dad will get to go home soon, but not until the second bag of IV fluid is empty. Do you want to sit on a chair next to the stretcher for a while?"

Danny looked at Leila and then back at his dad. "Could I play games on your computer instead?" he asked.

There was a moment of shocked silence, and then Quinn smiled, his eyes suspiciously bright as he pushed himself upright and swung his legs over the edge of the cart. "Get me a wheelchair," he demanded, swaying slightly as he struggled to stay upright. "Danny wants to play computer games in my office. I can get the rest of my IV fluids in there just as easily as lying here."

She was happy for Quinn. Really truly, happy for him. Clearly Danny's talking hadn't been just a passing phase. He was honestly doing better, seeming to have found his voice after all this time.

Jadon looked like he wanted to protest about Quinn

getting up, but the determined expression on Quinn's face must have made him realize it would be futile.

She knew she still had her stab-wound patient to return to, but couldn't help staring after them as Quinn and Danny made their way to Quinn's office, towing Quinn's IV pole.

There was no reason to be upset that they'd shut her out. Yet hadn't the night she and Quinn spent together meant anything? Obviously not to Quinn. The sharp edge of disappointment sliced at her heart as she headed into the arena.

Quinn still felt dizzy but he ignored the sensation, far too elated over Danny talking to care about himself.

His son had spoken. Not just once, but apparently several times. He'd never tire of hearing the sweet sound of Danny's voice.

He tried hard to hide his overwhelming joy and thankfulness as he wheeled along beside Danny. He was too afraid to make a big deal about Danny talking, much as he wanted to.

Instinctively, he knew that he should simply act as if Danny talking wasn't a major milestone. He could hear Nancy Adam's voice in the back of his mind, saying, "Keep doing whatever you're doing."

The move to Cedar Bluff had been the best decision he'd made. Nancy and the people of the town, including his son's classmates Charlie and Ben, had been wonderful in making them feel at home. Never once had Danny's classmates made fun of him for not talking.

Would Danny keep talking now that he'd started? A sudden doubt made his stomach clench. What if something traumatic happened, sending Danny back into silent mode?

No, don't borrow trouble, he told himself. Danny would continue to talk if he needed to. Hadn't Nancy claimed that Danny was expressing frustration at his limited ability to communicate? Surely he'd keep talking now that he'd started.

Quinn swallowed hard as he leaned over to log onto the computer. Sitting back, he gave Danny room to edge onto his chair, the walking cast on his leg making the movement awkward. He pulled the rolling chair as close to the computer as he could, so Danny could reach the keyboard.

"So what game are you going to play?" he asked, keeping his tone casual. He tried to hide how weak he still felt.

Danny lifted a shoulder in a half-shrug, his attention on the screen. He tried not to panic that Danny might be going back to his old ways. Just because Danny had started speaking, it didn't mean his son would suddenly become loquacious.

"This one," Danny finally said, double-clicking on the spider solitaire game.

His shoulders relaxed and Quinn couldn't help but smile. He still felt lousy, the flu bug still wreaking havoc in his bloodstream, but he wasn't about to complain. Not when he'd been given the gift of his son's speech.

He'd never complain again. He felt bad that he'd scared his son, but in the end things had worked out well. The humiliation of succumbing to flu in the first place and falling flat on his face in the parking lot was well worth it if Danny would keep talking.

As Danny played the game, Quinn's thoughts went back to Leila. He'd probably overreacted a bit when she'd offered to watch over Danny while he waited for his IV fluids to finish. Seeing Danny standing too close to Leila had freaked him out. He'd loved every minute of the night they'd spent together, but he didn't want to change anything else that might affect Danny.

Keep doing whatever it is you're doing.

He was going to concentrate on being a good father. On establishing a family-like atmosphere with Delores and Danny. He certainly wasn't going to add something as dramatic as a new woman into the picture.

He'd have to end his affair with Leila. Sure, maybe they could keep meeting in secret, but he knew that seeing her constantly in the ED would make things difficult. Besides, meeting only in secret wasn't fair to her.

The idea of never making love to her again made him feel as though a rock was pressing on his chest. He'd miss her. Very much. He still wanted her. But his needs weren't important. He simply couldn't afford to upset Danny.

Nothing was more important than his son.

Danny let out a disgusted sigh when he lost the game.

"Try again," Quinn advised. "We have a little more time yet before my IV fluids will be finished."

Without a word, Danny double-clicked on the game again. Quinn dropped his forehead into his hands, suddenly exhausted, feeling very much like he'd been run over by a cement truck.

He hated to ask for favors, but even once he was discharged, he wasn't going to feel good enough to drive home. And Delores was in no condition to pick them up.

No doubt about it, he was going to have to ask Leila for help. One last time.

Right before he told her they couldn't see each other anymore.

"Quinn?" At the sound of Jadon's voice he prised his eyes open. "I'm going to wheel you back into the ED. Your IV fluids are finished, but I'm not going to discharge you until your vital signs are stable."

Quinn scowled. "I'm sure they're fine."

Jadon cocked a brow. "Maybe. We'll see." He leaned over to release the brakes on Quinn's wheelchair.

"Danny? Shut off the computer now," he told his son.

"Why don't you let him stay for a while?" Jadon asked. "Your office is safe enough and we can come and get him once you're ready to go."

Danny glanced over at the adults. "Please?"

How could he deny his son anything when he asked so nicely? He'd never get tired of hearing Danny's voice. Ever. "No problem. But stay here, okay? No wandering around."

Danny nodded again, his attention already back on the game. Jadon wheeled Quinn back toward one of the rooms in the arena. "I bet you're happy he's talking," Jadon said.

"Yeah." A massive understatement.

"So what's going on with you and Leila?"

What? He stared at Jadon. "What do you mean? There's nothing going on."

Jadon's eyebrows rose in disbelief. "Who do you think you're kidding? I already know there was no lost bracelet. When you were lying unconscious in the middle of the trauma bay, she told us you'd spent the night at her house but had seemed fine when you left in the morning."

Quinn winced. "Ah, hell," he muttered. Now the whole world would know. There were no secrets in Cedar Bluff. None.

"Hey, none of my business," Jadon said, lifting a hand as if to ward off an attack. "But I was once sitting in your shoes, half in love with the best woman in the world but refusing to acknowledge it."

"I'm not in love with her," he said quickly, denying the sudden lurch in the vicinity of his heart. "We had a brief sexual fling, nothing more."

A footstep behind him made him freeze.

"I see you're feeling better, Quinn." Leila's voice, full of false cheerfulness, nearly made him wince again.

Talk about rotten timing.

He steeled himself to meet her gaze, nearly flinching at the wounded reproach in her eyes. He wanted to tell her he was sorry, that he hadn't meant for her to find out this way.

But nothing he could say would change the facts.

Their relationship—no, their brief liaison—was over.

"I am better." His voice sounded polite. Formal. As if they hadn't spent the night lost in the pleasure of making endless love. "Thanks."

She stared at him for a full minute, before giving a brief nod. "Good. Take care of yourself and Danny."

"I will." He clutched the arms of his wheelchair tightly to prevent himself from calling her back when she walked away.

"You are such a stupid ass." Jadon's tone betrayed his disgust.

Maybe.

He'd hurt Leila when he hadn't meant to. The expression of betrayal in her eyes would haunt him for a long time. And he still didn't have a ride home.

But Danny was talking again, sweet music to his ears. He had to accept his life as it was, no matter how much his heart ached.

CHAPTER THIRTEEN

LEILA blindly walked out of Quinn's room, his blunt words echoing over and over in her head.

We had a brief sexual fling, nothing more.

Tears burned her eyes, but she held them back, refusing to cry. Hadn't he warned her all he wanted was an affair right from the start? How stupid was she to let her emotions get involved when Quinn had made it perfectly clear he didn't want anything but sex?

This was her fault. She'd known all along lust wasn't love. And obviously those heated hours they'd spent together had really been nothing more than lust.

The realization made her feel sick. And not with flu.

She had patients to see. Work would help keep her grounded, just like it had after George had died. She could work with Quinn, keeping her distance. And if she couldn't, she had the option of leaving Cedar Bluff.

She didn't want to, but she could. She had no ties here anymore. None at all.

Leila left the ED, her path taking her past Quinn's office.

The door was ajar and Danny was inside, playing games on the computer.

Her footsteps slowed, and then stopped. After a moment's hesitation, she retraced her steps, pausing in the open doorway. "Hi, Danny. Having fun?"

The boy nodded somewhat absently, his attention on the game, until he abruptly let out a heavy sigh. "Rats. I lost again."

"Bummer." She ventured a little farther into the room, even though she knew Quinn wouldn't be happy she was there, talking to Danny. She suspected he didn't want her to get too close to his son, but she wasn't sure why. "I wanted to thank you again for helping out with your dad. You were very brave."

Danny abandoned the computer, swiveling back and forth on the rolling chair, his cast sticking out and his expression serious. "I was afraid he wouldn't wake up. Like my mom. I shaked her and shaked her but she didn't wake up."

Dear God. She tried not to look shocked. "That must have been really scary for you, Danny."

Danny bit his lip and nodded. "She died. My dad said she went to heaven to be an angel."

She'd died? Danny's mother had died? While Danny had been with her? She could just imagine the poor kid, trying over and over again to wake up his mom. Had he been all alone with his mom when she'd died? Was that the reason he'd stopped talking?

And was that the reason Quinn wasn't interested in anything more than an affair? Because he was still in love with his dead wife?

"I bet she's a wonderful angel," Leila said in a choked voice. "And I'm sure she's watching over you every minute."

"Uh-huh." Danny's gaze focused on a spot over her shoulder and she turned to see Quinn standing there, scowling at them. "Hi, Dad."

"Danny, we need to go. Seth is coming to pick us up."

"Cool." Leila handed Danny his crutches. He slid down from the chair and she put a hand on it to keep it steady for him. "Can I play with Ben today?"

"We'll see." Quinn still looked pale and none too steady, but the anger in his gaze, when he stared at her, was difficult to ignore.

For some reason, she hastened to defend herself. "Danny and I were just talking about how scared he was when you collapsed," she said, keeping her voice low so Danny wouldn't hear. "He was afraid you weren't going to wake up, like his mom didn't."

A muscle twitched at the corner of his jaw. "So now you know the truth. You know why Danny stopped talking eighteen months ago. Maybe he was traumatized when his mother died but, as you can see, he's better now. How dare you bring it up again, risking a serious setback?"

Shocked, she could only stare at him. "I didn't. Danny brought it up."

"Because you said something, I'm sure. Stay out of it, Leila," he said harshly. "Leave the past alone."

"Danny wasn't the only one traumatized," she argued, angry at the way he'd blamed her for pumping Danny for information. She really hadn't. And, besides, maybe if Quinn had opened up about the past she would have known the truth before now and could have avoided any possibility of a setback for Danny. "You were, too. You lost your wife. I told you my husband died, but you never said a word about being a widower as well."

"Leave it alone," he said, turning away to follow his son. "It has nothing to do with you."

She reared back as if he'd slapped her. Nothing to do with her? Why? Because she was nothing to him? Not even a friend? He walked away and she sucked in a hard breath, wishing she could chase after him, grab him by the shoulders and shake some sense into him. But she didn't move. All she could do was stand there, in his office, feeling even worse than before.

Quinn had spent the night with her but, other than giving her the pleasure of his body, he'd shared nothing else with her.

Nothing.

And, obviously, he planned to keep it that way.

Leila was on call, but the trauma room was quiet and when she finally ran out of work to do she headed home, knowing she lived only five minutes away if a trauma call did come in.

Her house was dark. Silent. Empty.

More empty than she remembered.

She checked her computer, and as always went to the reunion Web site first thing, but there was still no word from the woman who'd claimed to be her mother. Obviously, this Maylyn Aquino didn't have any proof that Leila was her daughter.

With a heavy sigh, she logged out of the reunion Web site. Nothing was going right for her. Not the possibility of finding her birth mother and certainly not the *sexual fling* she'd shared with Quinn. Unable to relax, she wandered around her small house, the unmistakable scent of Quinn seemingly following her everywhere she went.

In her bedroom, his musky scent was by far the strongest and in a fit of despair she quickly stripped the sheets off her bed, marched them to the laundry room and dumped them into the washing machine. Then she lit dozens of pine-scented candles, including several in her bedroom, determined to get rid of the haunting scent.

She didn't need any reminders of how stupid she'd been.

Stupid, so stupid to fall in love with him.

The knowledge came from nowhere and hit her hard, sucking the air from her lungs, nearly bringing her to her knees. Numb, she sank onto the sofa.

She loved Quinn.

When had it happened? How?

The love she'd shared with George had been so different. Gentle. Kind. A partnership, until he'd gotten so sick and then she'd cared for him until he'd died.

From the very beginning, being with Quinn had been nothing like the gentle caring she'd shared with her husband.

Yet the moment she'd seen Quinn crumpled on the ground next to his car, her heart had jumped into her throat. Panicked, she'd rushed to him, deathly afraid. Quinn had always been so strong, indomitable.

The passion between them had been earth-shattering. At least for her. Very different from what she'd had with George. Even after everything that had happened, she wanted Quinn. Knew she'd always want him.

She put a hand to the center of her chest, rubbing at

the ache as if it were a sore muscle she could massage better. There was no point in denying the truth—she loved him. With her whole heart and soul.

Too bad he didn't feel anything even close to love in return.

Physically, Quinn felt better after twenty-four hours. Emotionally, he was as irritable as a badger.

Danny was doing great. Quinn had experienced a rough moment when Ben had asked Danny, "How come you can talk now?"

He'd held his breath, praying that Danny wouldn't relapse back into silence, but his son had simply shrugged. "I just can."

"Oh. Okay." Ben seemed to accept Danny's answer at face value. Why, Quinn wasn't sure, and the boys continued to play as if nothing strange had happened.

Delores had wept when he'd told her the news. Tears of happiness, knowing that Danny had moved on from the trauma he'd suffered when Celeste had died, breaking through his wall of silence once and for all. He also called Nancy, who hadn't seemed nearly as surprised.

"I told you he'd talk when he was ready."

Quinn vaguely remembered hearing Danny shout out for someone to help his daddy. He'd hated knowing he'd scared Danny, yet he couldn't help being glad that the result had been Danny regaining his ability to talk.

Now, if only he could stop thinking about Leila, he'd be in great shape. Just fine and dandy.

He walked into the kitchen, not really paying attention to where he was going, thanks to another sleepless night thinking about Leila, when he stubbed his toe on the leg of the kitchen table.

"Dammit!"

"What is your problem?" Delores asked. "You haven't been yourself lately. You'd think you'd be happy now that you're feeling better and Danny is talking again."

"Nothing is wrong," he bit out between clenched teeth, reaching down to rub his big toe. "I am happy."

Delores gave a disgusted sniff. "You could have fooled me."

Maybe he was cranky. Mostly because he still didn't feel quite like his old self after that bout of flu. Plus he'd promised Seth he'd come to his wedding this evening and that he'd bring Danny so that Ben would have someone to hang out with. And to make matters worse, he'd agreed to have Ben stay overnight here with them for a sleepover so Seth and Kylie could have a proper wedding night.

Great for Danny and Ben, as the two were becoming best friends.

But not exactly the way he'd hoped to spend New Year's Eve.

Knock it off, he told himself harshly. Danny is talking, there's nothing more precious in the entire world than knowing his son was back to his former self.

The scars of the past had started to heal. He wouldn't risk opening them up again.

"What time are you leaving for the wedding?" Delores asked, pouring herself a cup of coffee and coming over to sit beside him at the table.

"Not until three-thirty or so." Quinn stood and helped

himself to a cup of coffee as well. Today coffee actually sounded good. "The wedding is at four o'clock with the reception immediately afterward." He tried to put on his happy face, although it wasn't easy, considering he'd have to face Leila at the wedding reception. "I'll have the boys home by ten o'clock at the latest."

"Great. Danny is so excited. It'll be good for them to spend more time together."

Yeah. The funny thing was, Danny didn't need him as much now that he was talking again. Or maybe it just seemed that way as he didn't have to read and interpret his son's sign language anymore.

The image of Danny teaching Leila sign language flashed into his mind.

He scrubbed his hands over his face. He owed her an apology for attacking her yesterday at the hospital. He'd been so angry when he'd overheard Danny telling her about his mother being in heaven as an angel that he'd been unable to see straight.

Worried about Danny having a relapse, he'd jumped all over her.

She'd said Danny had brought the subject up himself, and maybe he had. Leila had never been anything but kind to Danny. His son seemed close to her, especially after yesterday when he'd been sick. And that's what had bothered him most.

Because even if Leila was good with Danny, it didn't matter. He didn't want a wife. Didn't deserve a second chance.

"Quinn?" Delores said in an exasperated tone. "Are you listening?"

"What?" Guiltily, he lifted his head. No, he hadn't been listening. "I'm sorry, what did you say?"

"What do you think about me renting a couple of movies for the boys to watch when you get home tonight?" she repeated. "They can watch them until they fall asleep."

"Yeah. Sure. That's a great idea." He needed to pull himself together, and fast. Not only to get through the wedding tonight but for all the times in the future he'd have to work with Leila.

No, he didn't want a wife, but he was pretty sure Leila wanted the whole happily-ever-after package. A marriage like she'd had with her precious George.

The one thing he couldn't give her.

Quinn was forced to admit that Seth and Kylie's wedding wasn't too bad, as far as weddings went. It was small and simple, with Simon Carter as the best man and a paramedic friend of Kylie's as the maid of honor. Even he had gotten a little choked up when the two had solemnly exchanged vows they'd written themselves, their voices full of heartfelt love. And the way they'd included Ben in the ceremony, with the young boy standing at his mother's side, as Seth took on a family, not just a wife, was a nice touch.

Marriage did work for a few people and he suspected Seth and Kylie happened to be a pair of them.

His wedding to Celeste had been a formal affair, planned for over a year by Celeste and her mother. Any input from him hadn't been needed.

He'd thought he loved her, they'd seemed to want the same things out of life. He had plans to become the chief of emergency medicine and Celeste had been content to be a stay-at-home wife, and then, later, mom. But even within the first year, while they'd been trying to conceive Danny, he'd sensed something had been wrong.

Celeste hadn't been happy. He'd thought things would get better once she became pregnant, and they had for a while. But then Danny had been born and over the next two years things had progressively gotten worse.

Celeste had lashed out at him often, telling him he was a lousy husband and father. Her mood had swung from one extreme to the other and he'd tried to get her to accept help, but she'd refused. He'd suspected she was drinking, had tried to elicit help from her mother, but to no avail. His mother-in-law had jumped on every little thing that Celeste had claimed, as if it were gospel. The two of them ganging up on him hadn't helped.

He'd been able to tell Celeste was getting worse, instead of better. He'd suggested marriage counseling, but that had created the biggest fight of all. Celeste had raged at him, accusing him of not loving her anymore, and for a horrible moment he'd only stared at her, suspecting she was right.

The next day, he'd left for work as he always had. Halfway through his shift he'd called home, like he always had. But Celeste hadn't answered. Not at home and not her cell phone either.

He called her mother, who claimed she hadn't seen Celeste. He grew more and more worried. Where could she have gone with Danny? Then he received the call from the police.

Your wife is dead and your son is in shock. He won't leave her side.

Danny had apparently been screaming into the phone over and over again to the 911 operator until he'd been too hoarse to say any more. And then he'd stopped talking altogether.

Until now.

Quinn closed his eyes against the memories, putting the past back where it belonged, in the past. Celeste was gone and he and Danny had finally moved on.

Healed, in part, by the people of Cedar Bluff.

"Is it over now?" Danny asked in a loud whisper.

He nodded, smiling as Danny grimaced when Seth loudly kissed his bride. "Yes, it's over. After they're finished taking pictures, it'll be time for dinner."

"Good. I'm hungry."

Quinn caught sight of Leila, looking stunningly beautiful in an emerald-green dress that hugged her curves, the slit in the long skirt revealing her nicely shaped legs. Legs that had wrapped perfectly around his waist as he'd plunged deep.

Whoa. He pulled himself up short. Don't go there.

She saw him and gave him a brief nod, weary acceptance in her eyes, but then turned away, as if determined to keep her distance.

Jadon was right, he was an ass. At the very least he owed Leila an explanation. He couldn't just pretend that night of passion had never happened.

It was bad enough that it would never happen again.

He didn't get a chance to make his way over to her until after dinner. Ben and Danny had taken off as fast as Danny's walking cast had let him, searching for something to do, and Leila was finally standing off to the side, alone.

He made his way over to her. "Hi, Leila."

Her back went straight and she lifted her chin. "Hello, Quinn."

"Do you have a minute? I think we need to talk."

Her eyes widened in apprehension and she looked ready to bolt. "Um, no, I have to leave early, I'm on second back-up call and New Year's Eve is always a busy night."

"Please." He captured her hand with his. He could feel her pulse fluttering in her slender wrist. "I owe you an apology."

That seemed to surprise her, and she slowly nodded. "All right."

Now that he had her attention, he wasn't sure where to begin. He drew her a little farther away from the crowd, to a secluded corner of the room. "I'm sorry for jumping all over you yesterday in the hospital after you spoke with Danny."

"Look, about that, I swear I didn't bring up his mother, Quinn. He did. He told me he shook her and shook her but she wouldn't wake up."

He swallowed hard. "Yes. But the part that I hope and pray Danny doesn't ever have to know is that his mother didn't just get sick and die. She killed herself, by swallowing a full bottle of Valium."

"Oh, Quinn," Leila whispered, her eyes full of empathy.

Finish it, he told himself. *Tell her all of it.* "Leila, I care about you. That night we spent together was amazing. But I'm not interested in marriage. Celeste accused me of being a lousy father and a lousy husband. And then she took her own life rather than stay married to me." He forced himself to meet her gaze. Pouring out his deepest fears wasn't easy. "I've been given a second chance with Danny. I'm proving that I can be a good father. But I can't risk being a husband."

CHAPTER FOURTEEN

LEILA didn't know what to say. Clearly Quinn wasn't mourning his dead wife, at least not in the way she'd assumed.

The circumstances around his wife's death were horrible. Poor Danny. And poor Quinn. She couldn't imagine how awful they must have felt after Celeste had died.

But didn't Quinn and Danny deserve to move forward with their lives, too?

Quinn cared about her. His words had warmed her heart. The night they'd spent together hadn't been just about sex. But he also wasn't open to exploring a relationship either.

And suddenly, knowing that he cared, at least a little, made her realize she hadn't completely lost him. Not yet. And she'd fight to keep him if that's what it took. "Quinn, I'm not Celeste. Please, give me a chance. I love you."

He stared at her in surprised shock.

She gave his arm a hard shake, trying to snap him out of it. "Did you hear me? I love you."

His eyes widened and he took a hasty step backward, pulling out of her grasp. "No. Don't say that. You don't love me. You can't."

"Quinn." She reached for him, but he shook his head and stepped away.

"No. I can't do this. I'm sorry, Leila." He turned and disappeared into the crowd gathering on the dance floor in front of the DJ who was asking for the bride and the groom to start off the first dance.

She tried to find Quinn in the crowd, but couldn't. Her heart squeezed in her chest. Had he left? No, Danny was still there, on the dance floor, having abandoned his crutches. He was trying to imitate Ben's dance moves in spite of his bulky walking cast.

Quinn hadn't left, but he wasn't open to talking to her anymore either.

Her shoulders sagged and she ran her fingers through her hair. This was worse than she'd thought. This wasn't just about Quinn being protective of Danny. The problem was deeper, much deeper than that. It was Quinn himself, closing himself off to love. To having a future.

She collapsed into a chair and closed her eyes. What on earth could she say to him? How could she convince him to give their love a chance?

She wasn't sure there was a way to reach him. Especially as he hadn't admitted he loved her.

Maybe he wasn't capable of love. Other than for his son.

Despair sucked the air from her lungs, making her stomach cramp painfully.

This might not be a battle she was able to win.

* * *

Leila couldn't leave the wedding without saying good-bye to Seth and Kylie, and since they were entwined in each other's arms on the dance floor, she tapped her foot and waited for them to finish.

"Alyssa!" Ben shrieked, as he dashed across the room when Jadon and Alyssa walked in. They'd been at the ceremony, but had skipped dinner, going home to take care of the twins before returning to the reception.

"Hi, Ben," Alyssa greeted the boy, bending over to give him a big hug. "How are you?"

"Good. How're the twins?" he asked.

Alyssa laughed. "Growing like weeds."

Leila approached, glad to see Alyssa and Jadon were doing so well. She was sure that raising premature twin girls was trying, but the two of them still glowed with happiness. A happiness she envied.

"Who's your new friend?" Alyssa asked because Danny had followed Ben like a shadow.

"This is my friend Danny. He couldn't talk before but now he can."

Alyssa shot Jadon a puzzled look, before smiling at the boy. "Hi, Danny, it's nice to meet you."

Danny ducked his head shyly. Leila glanced around, looking for Quinn, but he was over at the bar, deep in conversation with Simon Carter.

"Danny is Quinn's son," Leila explained, placing a reassuring hand on Danny's shoulder.

"Quinn?" Alyssa asked with a frown. Then her eyes widened. "You mean Dr. Torres?"

"Yes, exactly." Leila remembered on Quinn's first day in the trauma bay how he'd jumped all over Alyssa, threatening to call Security as she hadn't been officially on duty when she'd helped out a coworker. "I see you remember him, but don't worry, Quinn Torres has mellowed out since that day he threatened to call Security on you. He's a great physician."

"Yeah, if you say so," Alyssa said doubtfully.

"Would you like something to drink?" Jadon asked, including Leila in his question.

"Just a caffeine-free ginger ale," Alyssa said with a deep sigh.

Leila smiled, knowing Alyssa couldn't drink while she was breastfeeding. "I'll have the same. I'm on call later," she said to Jadon.

"Be right back." He disappeared, heading over to the bar.

"Alyssa, will you dance with me?" Ben asked.

Alyssa looked surprised and pleased. "Well, certainly, Ben. I'd love to dance."

They walked onto the dance floor. Ben took both of her hands in his and then carefully stepped from side to side, his tongue sticking out between his teeth as he concentrated on not stepping on his partner's feet.

"Will you dance with me?" Danny surprised Leila by taking her hand in his.

She hesitated, knowing Quinn wouldn't like it, but then couldn't bring herself to refuse him. Not when his large dark eyes warily waited for her response. She smiled gently. "Of course, Danny. I'd love to dance with you."

She towered over Danny, and his movements were limited with his cast, but he was sweetly earnest in his attempt to dance with her, copying Ben's steps the best he could.

This was how great it could be, if Quinn would only give her a chance. She loved Quinn and already cared deeply about his son. Her eyes welled with tears, and she blinked them away, telling herself she'd leave right after this last dance.

Halfway through the song, Jadon came up behind Ben, tapping him lightly on the shoulder. "Hey, there, mind if I take over for a while?"

"I'll dance with you again, Ben, don't worry," Alyssa assured the boy.

"Okay." Ben relinquished control and allowed Jadon to sweep Alyssa close. Watching Jadon as he ardently kissed Alyssa made her want to cry all over again.

"Hey, Danny, mind if I cut in?"

Simon stood behind Danny and Leila had to swallow her disappointment because he wasn't Quinn.

"Sure," Danny said, seemingly relieved to be given the opportunity to hobble over to Ben.

She tried to smile. "Hi, Simon."

"Hi, yourself," he answered with a wide grin, taking her into his arms but not holding her too close. "You look gorgeous tonight, Leila."

"Thanks." She wished, not for the first time, that she'd been attracted to Simon. He was single, good-looking and a great guy.

But there had never been any spark of attraction between them. Simon was nice, but he wasn't the man she wanted.

She wanted Quinn.

Why had she fallen for the one man who didn't want anything to do with having a permanent relationship?

The DJ played another waltz and Simon kept right

on dancing, although she found herself subtly glancing around for Seth and Kylie. She was leaving right after this dance, regardless of where the bride and groom happened to be. If Seth and Kylie weren't around for her to say goodbye, too bad.

A wedding, especially one on New Year's Eve, was the last place to be when your heart was breaking.

Quinn sipped his drink, a dry martini, and watched his son ask Leila to dance.

His heart twisted painfully as they approached the dance floor, Danny's step uneven with the walking cast, knowing he was being ridiculous to be jealous of his six-year-old son. Yet they looked good together. His son liked Leila, he could tell. She was gentle with him, teasing him and making him laugh.

He'd been so adamant that Danny didn't need a mother, but maybe he was wrong. Danny was on the road to recovering from the trauma he'd suffered when Celeste had died.

As he watched Leila, another thought nagged at him. What if Leila decided to give up on him? What if she decided to move on with someone else? Like Simon Carter? Or Michael Hendricks?

Who Leila chose to see was none of his business. He'd walked away from her, told her they didn't have a future. Yet the more he stood there, imagining her turning to one of the single guys at Cedar Bluff like Simon or Michael, the angrier he got.

What in the hell was wrong with him? He didn't want a wife, but he wanted Leila. And he didn't want anyone else to have her either.

"I think I'll cut in on Ben," Jadon said. "The poor kid has a serious case of hero-worship for Alyssa, but with the twins home, we're lucky to have any time alone together. I want to dance with my fiancée."

"Good idea. I'll come with you and cut in on Danny," Simon chimed in.

Quinn sent him a sharp glance and Simon pretended to ignore him. He wanted to protest, to say, Back off, buddy, she's mine. But he kept his mouth shut. This was a free country; he couldn't stop Leila from dancing with whomever she chose. He couldn't do anything but watch helplessly as Jadon and Simon left him alone at the bar.

The two men wove through the crowd of dancers, each claiming their new partners. His jaw tense, Quinn tortured himself by watching, unable to tear his gaze from Simon and Leila.

They made a nice-looking couple. Leila was beautiful in her long green gown and Simon, formally dressed in his tux, was a perfect match for her, laughing down at something Leila was saying.

He had to restrain himself from marching over and planting his fist into Simon's laughing face.

Dammit, he shouldn't be torturing himself like this. But it was no use. He didn't want to see Leila with another man. Not now, not ever.

Because she belonged with him.

He loved her. The shocking realization hit hard. He loved her, but he was desperately afraid of being a husband and messing things up, the way everything had gone wrong with Celeste.

Yet at the same time he couldn't let Leila move on to someone else.

The slow dance finally ended and he tossed back the rest of his martini before crossing over to where couples were leaving the dance floor. Simon watched him approach, flashing him a knowing smirk, betraying the fact he'd purposefully asked Leila to dance just to get to Quinn. A fact that did not make him the least bit happy.

His warning glare told Simon to back off. He held her arm before she could disappear into the crowd. "Leila, wait."

She swung to face him, and when recognition dawned, her eyes darkened with apprehension. "Danny asked me to dance and I didn't want to disappoint him by refusing," she said in a rush.

"I know," he said, feeling like a jerk because it was clear she expected him to be angry. "I saw him ask you and I'm glad you didn't hurt his feelings. May I have the next dance?"

"I, uh, don't think so." She avoided his gaze. "I'm, uh, leaving. Gosh, where are Seth and Kylie? I keep missing them."

She was running away because he'd hurt her. Panic made him tighten his grip on her hand. "Leila, please. One dance."

She wanted to brush him off, he could tell, but she finally nodded and allowed him to lead her onto the crowded dance floor.

He pulled her into his arms, holding her close. She fit in his embrace perfectly. He wanted to kiss her, but she kept her head angled away from his, as if trying to keep a respectable distance between them.

"I'm so glad Danny's doing better," she murmured. "He seems to be talking all the time now."

"Yeah, and I'll never get tired of listening."

"No, I'm sure you won't." Her smile was brittle.

"Leila, I'm sorry."

"Don't be." Her chin lifted a notch. "I'm a big girl, I'll get over you."

But he didn't want her to get over him. He wasn't explaining himself well at all. "I'm sorry I hurt you," he said. "But I've already failed once at being a husband. Do you blame me for being cautious?"

Leila was quiet for a moment. "Did you ever think that it was Celeste who failed you?"

His head snapped back in surprise. What was she talking about? "It was my fault. She was depressed, but being with me, being married to me, made her worse."

"No." She looked up at him now. "You can't really believe that. A marriage takes two people. Your wife was sick, but she could have gotten help. She could have asked for a divorce. She had plenty of options."

"There aren't a lot of options when you're depressed, it's part of the disease." And looking back, he knew he had to take some accountability. "I wasn't home enough," he said, repeating the words Celeste had flung at him in bitter anger. "I didn't love her enough."

"Maybe you didn't," she agreed. "But we don't have control over our feelings. We can't make something out of nothing, no matter how much we want to."

He swallowed hard, knowing she was right. She'd nailed the source of the deep guilt he'd lived with. That he hadn't loved Celeste enough. Had wanted to help her to get better, but had been unable to love her the way she'd needed to be loved.

It was sobering to admit he hadn't loved Celeste the way he loved Leila.

"Besides, if you ask me, she didn't love you enough either. Or her son. She was obviously very sick, or she wouldn't have taken her own life, especially putting her own son at risk. Her death was a tragedy, but you must know it's not all your fault. You can't keep beating yourself up over her illness."

"I should have helped her." That much he firmly believed.

"Maybe, but she also had to want to help herself."

He drew a deep breath and let it out slowly, absorbing her words. He had tried to help her, but Celeste hadn't listened. She'd refused to go to counseling. He hadn't been able to force her into treatment, not without proving she was a danger to herself. And he hadn't known she had been until it had been too late.

Leila was right. He couldn't keep punishing himself for Celeste's death. But he was afraid of starting over. Of failing.

"I love you, Quinn," she told him. "And it doesn't matter if you return those feelings for me or not, I'll still love you. Now and forever."

His arms tightened around her. "I'm afraid," he admitted in a low voice.

She surprised him by smiling. "That's okay. Being in love is scary."

She was trying to make light of it, to help him relax, but so far it wasn't working. "I don't think you understand. I'm afraid I'll mess up. How do you know I'm not a bad husband?"

"How do you know I'm not a bad wife?" she countered.

Okay, now she was being ridiculous. "You had two wonderful years with George."

"Quinn, every marriage has its ups and downs, its problems and its celebrations. George and I were no exception. I loved him, but he wasn't perfect. And he thought I was obsessed with my past because I didn't know anything about who my parents are or what genes or prevalent diseases run in my family. And maybe he was right, as I've spent hours on the Internet, trying to find my birth mother." She sounded totally serious when she added, "Trust me, I'm no prize. I'm sure we'll both make mistakes. It's part of learning how to be partners."

"Partners," he murmured. The concept was foreign but hearing Leila say it with such conviction gave him hope. "I like the sound of that."

Her smile was tremulous. "Me, too."

He pulled her close. It was the eve of a new year and she'd just given him a new chance at love. "I love you, Leila. And I'm willing to spend my life proving it to you."

Her eyes misted. "You already have," she whispered.

EPILOGUE

QUINN pulled Danny close and straightened his small dress shirt. The boy squirmed, not too thrilled with the dressing-up part of his dad's plan.

"How come we have to look nice?" Danny wanted to know. "Leila already likes us, right?"

Quinn tried not to let on just how nervous he was. "Yes, she likes us. We dressed up to let her know how much we care."

Danny shrugged, his gaze still puzzled, and Quinn could tell his logic went right over his son's head. The doorbell pealed.

"She's here!" Danny headed over to open the front door.

He drew in a deep breath and let it out slowly. He wasn't nervous. Had no reason to be nervous because he did believe what he'd told his son. He was certain of Leila's love. And of his love for her.

But this was a big step. For him. Putting the past to rest once and for all.

He followed Danny into the living room, his heart swelling with love when he saw Leila smiling down at his son.

"Danny, you look so nice all dressed up."

"Thanks." Danny made a face that was mostly a grimace.

Quinn crossed over to Leila, brushing a light kiss on her mouth when he really wanted to haul her close and kiss her senseless. "Hi, Leila. Let me take your coat."

"Hi, Quinn." She kissed him back and then sniffed the air. "Mmm. Something smells delicious. Thanks for inviting me over for dinner. I had no idea you could cook."

"I'm full of surprises," he teased, although in truth he'd had to take a crash course in cooking from Delores, and he couldn't totally vouch for the meal he was about to serve, but he had done his best. One would think his Italian genes would help a little when making home-made lasagna.

"I helped toss the salad," Danny said loudly. "And me and Dad have a plan."

Quinn wanted to slap a hand over his son's big mouth. Their *plan* had been to wait until after dinner to serve Leila her engagement ring with dessert. But he suspected Danny wasn't going to be able to keep their plan a secret for much longer.

"A plan?" Leila sent him a confused look and nodded. "Well, it is good to have a plan when you're making a meal."

Now Danny looked confused, and Quinn made a quick decision. "Danny, I need you to help me in the kitchen for a minute. Leila, have a seat on the sofa. Would you like a glass of wine?"

"I'd love one, thanks."

Quinn practically dragged Danny into the kitchen.

"Okay, we're changing the plan. How about we give Leila the ring now and pop the question before dinner?"

"Yeah!" Danny readily agreed.

"I need to get her wine first." Quinn opened the bottle of wine, realizing his hands were sweating. Taking another deep breath, he swiped his damp palms on his slacks, told himself to calm down and then poured two glasses of wine before turning to Danny. "Do you have the ring?"

Walking on his cast without the crutches, Danny went over to the counter where they had the ring box discreetly hidden behind the chocolate cake, also made with Delores's help once Quinn had learned Leila had a weakness for chocolate. "Got it."

"Do you remember what you're going to say?" Quinn asked, even though they had rehearsed this part several times.

Danny nodded.

"Let's go, then." Quinn carried the wineglasses into the living room and sat down on the sofa next to Leila. He set their glasses on the table, and then gave Danny the signal.

Danny stood beside her. "Leila, me and my dad want to know if you'll marry us and be a family forever and ever?" Danny proposed exactly the way they'd rehearsed. But then he couldn't get the ring box open.

"Oh, Danny. Quinn." Leila's eyes filled with tears as she glanced at Danny and then back at him. "Of course I'll marry you and be a family with you."

Quinn gently tugged the ring box from Danny's hands, opened it and showed the ring to Leila. "I know it's not a traditional diamond, but Danny and I thought the deep amethyst matched your eyes perfectly. But if you don't like it as an engagement ring, we can get a diamond, too."

"No, I love this one," she said with a tearful sniff and a watery smile. "It's beautiful."

He and Danny exchanged grins. Quinn took out the ring and gently slipped it on her finger. "Leila, I promise to be the best husband I can be. I wanted to propose to you today, so we can start off the new year and our new life together."

Tears slipped down her cheeks but as she was smiling, he wasn't too worried. "New beginnings sound wonderful. I promise to be a good wife, too." She reached over to pull Danny close. "And a good mother, for Danny and for any other children we decide to have."

Quinn knew that the decision to have more children hadn't been easy. Leila had just begun to correspond with her birth mother. He hoped, for her sake, they'd find a way to build some sort of relationship.

"I'm glad you're going to marry us," Danny said, giving her a hug and a kiss. "I love you."

"I love you, too." Leila returned his son's embrace and then smiled at Quinn. "I love both of you."

Her words, her heartfelt belief didn't make him nervous at all, because being with Leila felt right. New beginnings, just like she'd said. He pulled her close for a proper kiss, secure in the knowledge that true partners working together could make a marriage work.

Promising a lifetime of happiness.

0909 Gen Std HB

ROMANCE

The Billionaire's Bride of Innocence	Miranda Lee
Dante: Claiming His Secret Love-Child	Sandra Marton
The Sheikh's Impatient Virgin	Kim Lawrence
His Forbidden Passion	Anne Mather
The Mistress of His Manor	Catherine George
Ruthless Greek Boss, Secretary Mistress	Abby Green
Cavelli's Lost Heir	Lynn Raye Harris
The Blackmail Baby	Natalie Rivers
Da Silva's Mistress	Tina Duncan
The Twelve-Month Marriage Deal	Margaret Mayo
And the Bride Wore Red	Lucy Gordon
Her Desert Dream	Liz Fielding
Their Christmas Family Miracle	Caroline Anderson
Snowbound Bride-to-Be	Cara Colter
Her Mediterranean Makeover	Claire Baxter
Confidential: Expecting!	Jackie Braun
Snowbound: Miracle Marriage	Sarah Morgan
Christmas Eve: Doorstep Delivery	Sarah Morgan

HISTORICAL

Compromised Miss	Anne O'Brien
The Wayward Governess	Joanna Fulford
Runaway Lady, Conquering Lord	Carol Townend

MEDICAL™

Hot-Shot Doc, Christmas Bride	Joanna Neil
Christmas at Rivercut Manor	Gill Sanderson
Falling for the Playboy Millionaire	Kate Hardy
The Surgeon's New-Year Wedding Wish	Laura Iding

0909 Gen Std LP

OCTOBER 2009 LARGE PRINT TITLES

ROMANCE

The Billionaire's Bride of Convenience	Miranda Lee
Valentino's Love-Child	Lucy Monroe
Ruthless Awakening	Sara Craven
The Italian Count's Defiant Bride	Catherine George
Outback Heiress, Surprise Proposal	Margaret Way
Honeymoon with the Boss	Jessica Hart
His Princess in the Making	Melissa James
Dream Date with the Millionaire	Melissa McClone

HISTORICAL

His Reluctant Mistress	Joanna Maitland
The Earl's Forbidden Ward	Bronwyn Scott
The Rake's Inherited Courtesan	Ann Lethbridge

MEDICAL™

A Family For His Tiny Twins	Josie Metcalfe
One Night With Her Boss	Alison Roberts
Top-Notch Doc, Outback Bride	Melanie Milburne
A Baby for the Village Doctor	Abigail Gordon
The Midwife and the Single Dad	Gill Sanderson
The Playboy Firefighter's Proposal	Emily Forbes

NOVEMBER 2009 HARDBACK TITLES

ROMANCE

Ruthless Magnate, Convenient Wife	Lynne Graham
The Prince's Chambermaid	Sharon Kendrick
The Virgin and His Majesty	Robyn Donald
Innocent Secretary...Accidentally Pregnant	Carol Marinelli
Bought: The Greek's Baby	Jennie Lucas
Powerful Italian, Penniless Housekeeper	India Grey
Count Toussaint's Pregnant Mistress	Kate Hewitt
Forgotten Mistress, Secret Love-Child	Annie West
The Boselli Bride	Susanne James
In the Tycoon's Debt	Emily McKay
The Girl from Honeysuckle Farm	Jessica Steele
One Dance with the Cowboy	Donna Alward
The Daredevil Tycoon	Barbara McMahon
Hired: Sassy Assistant	Nina Harrington
Just Married!	Cara Colter & Shirley Jump
The Italian's Forgotten Baby	Raye Morgan
The Doctor's Rebel Knight	Melanie Milburne
Greek Doctor Claims His Bride	Margaret Barker

HISTORICAL

Tall, Dark and Disreputable	Deb Marlowe
The Mistress of Hanover Square	Anne Herries
The Accidental Countess	Michelle Willingham

MEDICAL™

Posh Doc, Society Wedding	Joanna Neil
Their Baby Surprise	Jennifer Taylor
A Mother for the Italian's Twins	Margaret McDonagh
New Boss, New-Year Bride	Lucy Clark

1009 Gen Std LP

NOVEMBER 2009 LARGE PRINT TITLES

ROMANCE

The Greek Tycoon's Blackmailed Mistress	Lynne Graham
Ruthless Billionaire, Forbidden Baby	Emma Darcy
Constantine's Defiant Mistress	Sharon Kendrick
The Sheikh's Love-Child	Kate Hewitt
The Brooding Frenchman's Proposal	Rebecca Winters
His L.A. Cinderella	Trish Wylie
Dating the Rebel Tycoon	Ally Blake
Her Baby Wish	Patricia Thayer

HISTORICAL

The Notorious Mr Hurst	Louise Allen
Runaway Lady	Claire Thornton
The Wicked Lord Rasenby	Marguerite Kaye

MEDICAL™

The Surgeon She's Been Waiting For	Joanna Neil
The Baby Doctor's Bride	Jessica Matthews
The Midwife's New-found Family	Fiona McArthur
The Emergency Doctor Claims His Wife	Margaret McDonagh
The Surgeon's Special Delivery	Fiona Lowe
A Mother For His Twins	Lucy Clark

millsandboon.co.uk Community

Join Us!

The Community is the perfect place to meet and chat to kindred spirits who love books and reading as much as you do, but it's also the place to:

- Get the inside scoop from authors about their latest books
- Learn how to write a romance book with advice from our editors
- Help us to continue publishing the best in women's fiction
- Share your thoughts on the books we publish
- Befriend other users

Forums: Interact with each other as well as authors, editors and a whole host of other users worldwide.

Blogs: Every registered community member has their own blog to tell the world what they're up to and what's on their mind.

Book Challenge: We're aiming to read 5,000 books and have joined forces with The Reading Agency in our inaugural Book Challenge.

Profile Page: Showcase yourself and keep a record of your recent community activity.

Social Networking: We've added buttons at the end of every post to share via digg, Facebook, Google, Yahoo, technorati and de.licio.us.

www.millsandboon.co.uk